IMPRINT

Jo Ann Jury

ISBN 978-1-943650-66-8

Cover art by Tina Haldiman.

Published by BookCrafters, Parker, Colorado.
www.bookcrafters.net

I want to thank all those who believed in me. Especially, Barb, my partner and staunchest supporter who showed me all things were possible. My friends, Tina and Denise, for their advice, enthusiasm and encouragement. And to fellow author, Dianne Zimmerman who inspired me to fulfill my lifelong dream.

Chapter 1

It was a day full of promise, but it did not deliver. For Arthur Murdoch it was a day of disappointment he would not dismiss as he had done so many times in the past. This time there would be a price someone must pay but he hadn't worked out the details.

Just this morning he had sized up his appearance in the mirror to assess his professional image. Did he look the part of CEO? At 5'10" he wasn't as tall as he would like, but he wasn't a shorty either. Clean shaven, nice neat professional haircut sprinkled with just enough gray to look mature but not old. He could stand to lose a few pounds, maybe ten or fifteen. He certainly dressed the part, using the same tailor as the current CEO, Mr. Martin Carver, his father-in-law.

He then eagerly left for work and away from his insipid wife. How does one talk incessantly when one has absolutely nothing of value to say? She was the boss' daughter and the final step of the plan to gain control of the company when "daddy" retired. All the ass kissing, all the long hours, all the sacrifices, all for naught. The old man had handed the reigns to the annoying, loudmouth bully of a man who ran production. So what if he knows how to build a thingamajig and calibrate a whatchamacallit, neither qualifies you to handle the complexities of running a multimillion dollar company. Yet Carver Industries was now his to run. Run into the ground, Arthur imagined.

Later that evening, he delivered the bad news to his wife, Marion. For the first time in their five year marriage he actually enjoyed listening to her ranting and raving. She was as angry about the situation as he was, and her points of contention were the very same he had been complaining about for months. Perhaps she actually listened to him after all. Then she stopped him in his tracks.

"I guess now we have to wait for Daddy to die before we get what is rightfully ours," Marion Murdoch stated.

Why wait? was Arthur's spontaneous response that he was fortunate not to have said aloud. The evening went on for Marion with alternating moments of "what's on TV?" and "why is daddy being such a jerk?" but Arthur was simply consumed all night with his earlier thought of "why wait."

His sleepless night ended with his daily trip to the office. He really couldn't fathom why he would continue to work there when his future had been so abruptly derailed the day before. But it's what people do. It's what Arthur Murdoch had done for the duration of his adult life. If it wasn't bad enough that he had his hopes crushed personally by Mr. Carver yesterday, today he had to attend the meeting where the formal announcement of his successor would be made to the other execs and department heads. Then he would have to smile and congratulate Mr. Bully man.

Perhaps, while everyone was high fiving the new boss, Arthur could sidle up to the old boss with a letter opener and slit his throat. Or excuse himself from the meeting just in time to avoid the catastrophic explosion from the bomb he placed under Carver's chair. A snipers bullet. A poisoned yogurt cup. These were just a few of the death scenes Arthur envisioned during the course of the painful meeting. But with each new imaginary murder Arthur devised, there was a part of his calculating mind that would analyze and measure the flaws of that plan and discard it as unfeasible. More to the point, he would get caught.

In the days that followed, Arthur found his mind wandering into dark places. His thoughts were more scattered than he was accustomed to. One such meandering landed him in a hole of self-pity and depression. His world was crumbling. His career just hit a brick wall. His marriage was a sham and he had no real friends.

So ordinary, he thought, to be experiencing a mid-life crisis. He thought himself above that mundane, introspective, common man bullshit.

His marriage was always a part of his master plan

but it was not without its moments. When they met, he was struck by her ability to navigate a room with ease and people genuinely liked her. Arthur's best hope was to not get asked to leave but usually they just politely withdrew themselves from any conversations with Arthur they had inadvertently been drawn into. It used to bother him that people seemed repulsed by him but not so much anymore. At some point he realized he didn't want to talk to them any more than they wanted to talk to him.

But Marion did not retreat when circumstances landed her next to him at the company Christmas party. A modestly attractive redhead, she spoke fluent small talk but it didn't really matter what she was saying, it was just that she was saying it to him. She was clearly not repulsed by him and that alone was an endearing quality, although it shouldn't be.

Oh yes, I married her because she didn't run away in disgust. Isn't that adorable, Arthur thought to himself. He didn't know until the next day that she was the boss' daughter and that was the cherry on top. Thank goodness for that cherry or he would have smothered her with a pillow by now. Arthur occasionally wondered if he hadn't so quickly latched on to her as a means to an end to gain control of the company, then maybe, just maybe, their relationship stood a chance at being something real.

But that was the past and it had no place in the here and now and Marion had not made it any easier by having an affair. He tolerated the affair because he just didn't care enough about her to care about who she was sleeping with. Plus it was with a woman, how lame is that? They probably take turns blathering about nonsense which perhaps saves Arthur from hearing even more minutia than he already has to endure.

In light of the current situation he began to wonder if perhaps someone did know about the affair. Would they think him stupid for not knowing about it or weak for tolerating it...or both?

Suddenly what he had tolerated for months was now a possible contributing factor in his current predicament. If Mr. Carver knew Marion was having an affair and thought Arthur was oblivious to it how could Arthur be expected to be aware of potentially damaging business dealings? How could he control the company if he can't even control his own wife? Certainly Carver would have said something or maybe he blamed Arthur and this was the punishment. "How dare he blame me for his evil spawn and her cunt of a lover?" Arthur said quietly while staring into his bourbon.

"Did you say something honey?" Marion asked. "Dinner's ready."

Arthur was momentarily startled and grunted in response.

Chapter 2

Marion sipped her morning tea as they sat down to breakfast. She thought about Arthur, her father, and the company, and even though it angered her, it was not where her focus was right now.

Arthur's obsession with work left no time for her. For several years she watched his interest in her dwindle to silent tolerance.

Marion always felt that money was a contributing factor in Arthur choosing to marry her. Most of the time she could convince herself that money finished a distant second place behind love.

And she was not without guilt. She wanted an easy life where money was never an issue. Growing up a single child in a family of means made her accustomed to a certain lifestyle that she was not willing to relinquish. It made sense to marry Arthur, he was an upandcomer who seemed destined to run the company someday. Marion felt it was difficult to criticize his motives when hers were less than stellar.

She envisioned a couple of kids, a housekeeper, a nanny, and a cook, leaving plenty of time for shopping and social events. All that was coming to fruition until her pregnancy. Marion was ecstatic and Arthur was excited at the prospect of fatherhood.

Just a few weeks into the pregnancy, Marion appeared to have a miscarriage. It turned out to be an ectopic pregnancy, or tubal pregnancy. She was rushed into surgery where her Fallopian tube was removed, terminating the pregnancy. Afterward the doctor told her it was unlikely that she would get pregnant again and even if she did, it would probably be ectopic as well.

Something was lost between her and Arthur after that. First, the joy of a new life forever bonding them as a family, then suddenly a void that would never be filled.

It takes a great deal of effort to come back from something like that and neither of them were up to the task. Marion couldn't bear to talk about it, and Arthur didn't want to talk about it. Talking about his feelings was never Arthur's forte. So Arthur started working more and Marion started looking elsewhere for affection.

This was not much of a marriage, but it was a commitment she chose. A commitment she had no intention of abandoning. And no, her relationship with Victoria did not count as being unfaithful. Victoria was just a woman who made her feel special. A woman who listened. A woman who cared about her needs. A woman who made her feel loved. Marion gasped as she realized this did count as an affair. Suddenly her feelings toward

Vic felt more like love than friends-with-benefits. This thought startled her into the reality of Arthur actually talking to her.

"Should I be worried about the food?" Arthur sneered.

"What? I don't...no, what?" a confused Marion responded.

"The food. You've just been staring at it, not eating it. Is it poison? Are you trying to poison me bitch?" Arthur said sharply.

"Don't you call me that EVER. Say it again and I might just do it," Marion snapped.

Arthur was as stunned by her reply as she was. "Sorry, rough week," he said apologetically.

"I just don't like being called that word. You know Jeffrey used to call me that on a regular basis," Marion rattled on. "You remember Jeffrey hon, he was the guy I was engaged to before we met. He was a pilot, you know, commercial jets. He used to take me with..."

Arthur flipped a switch in his head and heard her no more.

Arthur spent the day hearing the chatter of what a great choice Jankowski was for CEO and all the perfunctory congratulations. This was unbearable. The notion of killing Carver seemed more necessary than ever but along with that notion existed the fear of being caught. It wasn't as if he was filled with an internal struggle, or any kind of moral dilemma, he should have been, but he was not. Arthur had no objection to murder just a profound objection to life in prison. He had been mulling it over for days now and he knew that it was time he took control of his future by taking control of the company.

Mr. Carver's last day of work was less than a month away. If he were to die in that time, well, as the only child, Marion would inherit it all and she would immediately install him as CEO. Not a complicated scenario...kill the bastard, don't get caught and let the rest happen as a simple matter of course. No problem with the first step but the not getting caught was going to be tricky. Arthur was a meticulous man and after reviewing each plan he devised he would always come to the conclusion that a reasonably intelligent detective would figure it out.

But what if he could achieve his goal without the risk?

Perhaps he could convince Carver to change his mind if he explained the folly of relinquishing control of the company to Mr. bully man, Stan Jankowski. Maybe Carver would see the light.

Throw in some hints as to Arthur's qualifications for the job and voila, job done. It was a long shot but the alternative is what...continue working at a job with the hope that someday another opportunity to seize the reins presents itself? Continue to endure a marriage that makes him nauseous? Both options are unacceptable.

Arthur made the call. "Martin, how are you doing tonight, sir?"

"I'm fine but I'm expecting a call from London momentarily.

What's on your mind, Art?" Martin Carver replied.

Arthur hated being called Art. Art is something you hang on a wall and forget about. My name is Arthur, he thought, but didn't dare say.

"Listen, I know you're heading to Dallas on Monday for that meeting but I was hoping to talk to you about some concerns I have regarding the transition." Arthur spoke in his best business casual tone so as not sound too aggressive.

"Well, Alice left for her sister's this morning so I'm on my own for the weekend. Lots of golf planned but you could drop by Sunday evening," Martin said.

They wrapped up the conversation and the wheels were officially set in motion.

Marion gave her usual excuse for being gone for hours on a Saturday...shopping. And she didn't have to worry about coming home empty handed. Arthur wouldn't even notice, but if he did ask, Marion knew that she could just start talking about not being able to find what she was looking for and a detailed description of her search and Arthur would just zone out.

She pulled up to the cafe and saw Victoria was already there. Marion was mildly upset that Vic was seated at an outdoor table. Easy for her, she's not the one with the husband and reputation to protect. This meeting was a little different than before in light of the revelation of discovering her feelings for Victoria were deeper than she had allowed herself to believe.

Marion backed away from the usual welcoming hug. Too many witnesses. It was doubtful any of her friends would be visiting this part of town but you never know. The Central West End was an eclectic neighborhood, artsy, sidewalk cafes, tattoo parlors, people walking their dogs. Hippies, preppies, goths, three-piece suits... you'll see it all in the Central West End.

Victoria Campo was a tall lean woman in her mid-twenties. Her short blond hair was buzzed close on the side with sweeping bangs.

"Good morning." Vic gently reached for her hand on the table but Marion withdrew hers.

"Hardly. It's two in the afternoon. Were you out partying all night?" Marion said rather sharply.

"Whoa! All I said was good morning, and I get a boatload of attitude." Vic barked. "I don't need this kind of..."

"I'm sorry hon, I'm sorry. Forgive me," Marion pleaded. "It's just that...oh, nevermind. You don't want to hear my problems."

"Sure I do," Vic said sympathetically. But it was a lie. She did NOT want to hear about Marion's problems.

Marion began retelling the events of the week, sparing no details. Vic is such a good listener, Marion thought.

Does she really think I have any interest in the life of my lovers' husband? Vic pondered.

When Marion had finished with the family crisis story she moved the conversation to more intimate thoughts.

"I've missed you," Marion sighed.

"I've missed you too," Vic replied but thought well, *I've missed the sex at least.* She decided to keep that thought to herself.

"I've been thinking a lot about us lately," Marion began. "I think I underestimated how much I care about you. I mean I think, I may, um, I'm pretty sure I love you."

Holy crap! Vic wasn't sure if her facial expression reflected the shock but it might have. Surely Marion was expecting a response of endearment culminating with an "I love you too" but Vic couldn't bring herself to say it. Instead, a rather bland "I see" is all she could muster.

"I see? I pour out my heart to you and all you can say is, I see?" Marion said disappointedly.

"You caught me off guard. This has been a casual relationship from the beginning and now you throw love in the mix. What did you expect?"

"Well certainly not 'I see'. And what the hell do you mean by casual relationship? Like, hi how are you.... let's fuck....thanks I'll see you around? Is that all I am to you?" Disappointment had turned to hurt with a splash of anger.

"No, that's not what I meant," Vic said. *Well kinda*, Vic thought. "No, that's not at all what I meant." Despite her defense there was no consoling Marion at this point and Vic saw this as the end. She wasn't heartbroken but she did feel a sense of loss.

The conversation got heated as Marion made a bit of a scene. Vic did not like her jilted lover act, not one bit. In the end Marion walked away in a huff as the other guests tried not to watch.

But parked across the street someone was watching very intently. Arthur snapped a couple more photos before driving away unnoticed.

Chapter 3

It was 7:30 and Arthur was mentally preparing for his meeting with Carver. He grabbed a bottle of Carver's favorite single malt scotch that he had in the liquor cabinet. Might as well score some positive points with him right off the bat. You think Jankowski knows his favorite brand? Not likely. He told Marion he was going out but she was watching her favorite show so she barely acknowledged his announcement. Normally he would not think twice about whether he gave her a good excuse but this time he wondered if he should have elaborated on his reason for going out. Could it be guilt? When he got to his car he immediately noticed his front driver's side tire was flat. "You've got to be kidding," Arthur mumbled. No time to call AAA so he quickly decided he would just take Marion's car.

He arrived at "the big house" as he not so fondly called it. Carver was most assuredly the warden.

Martin greeted him at the door. "Art, come on in. I was just about to pour myself a drink, join me."

"Well, then my timing is perfect." Arthur showed him the bottle he brought.

Martin smiled in approval, "Perfect indeed."

Never having been good at small talk Arthur got straight to the point. "I'm not sure Jankowski is up to the task of running the company."

"Well I am," Martin said dismissively.

That was quick. In his usual style he just shut Arthur down without discussion, but Arthur was not to be denied his say. "He hasn't the experience and his management style is weak. He doesn't have the firm hand that is needed to fill your shoes." Arthur pressed on, "He's never been out of the production side of things. I doubt he's ever read a financial statement before, much less understood it."

Unfazed Martin replied, "I am well aware of his weaknesses or rather I was aware of them. We've been working together for months in preparation for this transition."

"I see." Arthur was livid. He's been working his ass off trying to convince Martin that he was the man for the job and all the while Martin was grooming Jankowski.

"Here's the thing, Art." Martin continued, "I know you were hoping for the job but you are too valuable right where you are. This really is the best thing for all of us." Carver turned and started to walk away in one last dismissive gesture.

Arthur couldn't believe his ears. This was not the best thing for him. "You arrogant fuck!" Arthur shouted.

Without thought Arthur grabbed a wine bottle off the bar. Holding it by the neck he leapt to his feet. Then in one swift motion he wielded the bottle over his head bringing it down hard on the back of Martin's head. He crumpled to the floor like a marionette whose strings had been cut. Carver lay motionless on the floor while Arthur stood motionless above him.

All the different plans he had devised were all thrown out the window. All the means by which he would get away with it were useless as well. Now he was faced with the spontaneous task of covering his tracks. The job is done, now what? Fingerprints, Arthur wiped the bottle clean. He tried to retrace his steps and wipe down everything he touched. Then he realized it was unnecessary. He came over to his father-in-law's house frequently so it would be expected for his fingerprints to be there.

Maybe he should make it look like a robbery. This seemed logical; otherwise the police would assume it was an invited guest. This would make for a relatively short suspect list and Arthur would clearly be on it.

Just as Arthur was set to ransack the place he heard a groan. It was Martin, and then Arthur saw his arm move slightly. He wasn't dead. For a brief moment, Arthur felt relieved. No murder, no cover up needed. But that moment came and went as reality set in. There was no explaining this as an accident. He couldn't tell Martin 'sorry I accidentally knocked you unconscious with a wine bottle.' Then his already damaged career would be over. Fairly certain attacking the boss is grounds for dismissal. Then there's the law. Martin would probably involve the police, probably press charges and Arthur would probably go to prison. All those probably's led to one conclusion...finish the job.

Arthur glanced around the room looking for answers. Answers in the former of a murder weapon. The obvious choice was right in front of him, Martin's gun collection. There were a dozen guns in the cabinet, any one of which would do. *Where would the key be?* Arthur thought. He checked behind the bar. He left the room and checked the desk in Martin's office, no luck. He went back to the game room to find Martin staggering to his feet. Arthur grabbed the handles to the gun cabinet doors in the hopes that he could force it open. He pulled hard and nearly fell over. The damn thing was unlocked! Before he could select a gun he felt the full weight of Martin's body slam him into the cabinet. Arthur quickly regained his balance, whirled around and pushed back. Clearly Martin was disoriented from the earlier blow as he wobbled backward haphazardly falling into a chair.

Arthur grabbed a gun, a small caliber pistol that he knew he could handle. Not thinking about bullets Arthur aimed and fired. It was loaded, but Arthur missed. Sensing the obvious urgency Martin leapt out of his chair charging Arthur. But Arthur shot again and again hitting his target three times. Martin crashed to floor.

Arthur watched for any sign of life but there was

none. There was, however, a great deal of blood. Arthur checked Martin's pulse, there was no question, he was absolutely dead.

Now Arthur was back to the task at hand. It had only been minutes since he first contemplated covering his tracks, but he seemed infinitely more calm. He had to act quickly. No telling if a neighbor heard the shots or if Alice was due home tonight.

Arthur pocketed the gun. He had no idea if fingerprints would show up on clothes so he did his best with bar towel to wipe off where he pushed him and where he touched Martin to roll him over and take his pulse. He thought about taking a few things to solidify the burglary story but his fear of being discovered took over. He stuffed the towel in his pocket and bolted out the front door.

Taking care not to draw suspicion, he drove away slowly. He wanted to go home, have a drink and sit quietly while the adrenaline subsided but Marion was still up and he was in no mood for that. So he drove for hours. With every minute the fear of getting caught was being replaced by the satisfaction of killing the man who cheated him out of what, in Arthur's mind, was his destiny. It was a point of pride now. *I killed him. I secured my future. I am in control now dammit! How's that make you feel Martin? Oh wait, you're fucking dead!* Arthur reveled to himself with a wry smile on his face.

Arthur pulled into his garage just after one. Marion was sound asleep as he climbed into bed. The adrenaline was wearing off but his thoughts were still racing. He replayed the events of the evening over and over again. Did he remove the evidence thoroughly? Yes, he wiped down the gun, brought it home and stashed it in the garage. He probably should have gotten rid of it but the risk of being seen or having someone find it was too high. The towel he threw away at a gas station in a sketchy neighborhood. Was that it? Throw away a towel and hide a gun and call it a day? Hopefully, yes. Then Arthur would run it through his head all over again. After several hours he finally fell asleep.

Chapter 4

Marion Murdoch literally woke up with a bang. It seemed too preposterous to be real but too real to be a dream. Her instincts told her to wake Arthur and tell him. Tell him what? As she gathered her thoughts she knew something was askew. She grabbed the baseball bat that she kept in the closet and went to check the house. If there was a burglar who shot her father...Marion gasped as she realized that's exactly what she dreamt. She had shot her father and he was dead. As crazy as that seemed, the dream was becoming more and more vivid and extremely detailed. This was unlike any dream she'd ever had.

Most dreams are fragmented with random nonsensical bits and pieces. This was a story, start to finish, and it ended with her killing her father. But it was just a dream, wasn't it?

Marion was still in a fog so it was time for some coffee. Arthur was still asleep which was unusual at this hour. He should be up and getting ready for work but she was glad as she was no mood to talk to him. As details became clear Marion was forced to entertain the idea that there was at least a touch of reality embedded in this dream. Perhaps it was just symbolism in play. All of the anger at her father over the company coming out in a death wish. Suddenly she recalled her comment about waiting for daddy to die. That must be it, just a fantasy that invaded my subconscious.

As she was starting to believe the fantasy scenario the doorbell rang. "Who on earth is at my door this early in the day" Marion said to herself. She opened the door.

"Mrs. Murdoch?" the woman inquired.

"Yes," Marion replied.

"I'm Detective Bailey. This is Detective Schwartz. May we come in?"

Marion stood silent, her mind swirling with disturbing thoughts. Thoughts she dare not speak. She gestured them inside without saying a word.

"Your father is Martin Carver, correct?" Det. Bailey asked. Marion nodded.

"There is no gentle way to put this, Mrs. Murdoch, but your father was found dead in his home this morning," Gwen Bailey said in a mildly sympathetic tone.

Marion was understandably shocked but for more reasons than the detectives might assume. "What?" was all that came out of her mouth.

"Apparently the housekeeper found the body, uh, your father, when she came in to work today," Det. Schwartz added.

"How?" Marion spoke her second word.

"He was shot several times in the chest and stomach," Schwartz replied.

Bailey gave Schwartz a sharp look of disgust as that was way too much information to throw at a daughter who just lost her father. More importantly, keeping details close to the vest is essential when a murder investigation is just beginning.

Marion couldn't believe what was happening. It was not a dream. It was her own memories. The truth hit her. *I killed daddy,* Marion accepted this fact but said nothing.

"We've not been able to reach Mrs. Carver, she was not at home," Bailey continued. "I was hoping you could help in that regard."

Marion felt a sudden sadness in her heart. Mother will be devastated. "Oh yes, Aunt Jean. She's at Aunt Jean's." Marion wondered as she spoke if she sounded sufficiently upset so as to avoid suspicion. She then made a conscious effort to make eye contact with the detectives. Failure to do so makes you look guilty or lying or something. Marion had seen that on some TV show. "Do you want the number or should I call her?"

"If you have the address we'll take care of it," Bailey stated.

"Of course."

As Marion walked away she realized Arthur was still asleep and still unaware of what was happening. She needed him to be there. She couldn't trust herself another minute with police. When she looked in the bedroom, Arthur wasn't there. She heard the shower and stepped into the bathroom. "Arthur, I need you now. The police are here. Please hurry!"

Arthur dropped the soap and his heart skipped several beats.

The cops are already here. How could they know already? *Breathe, breathe*, Arthur told his body, but in his shock he forgot to respond to Marion.

He hurriedly uttered the most logical question. "Why are the cops here?" he said as casually as he could manage.

"Just come into the living room as soon as possible," Marion implored.

Marion returned to the living room with the address and phone number of her mother's sister. She didn't know what to do or say now which made her even more glad to see Arthur join them, but she did not want to tell him what was going on. When Arthur asked she signaled to Det. Bailey with a nod and a pleading look.

While Arthur spoke to the police Marion just sat there, too distraught to participate in the conversation. *I killed my father*, the thought was echoing in her head. *I hit him on the head with a wine bottle and then I shot him. Why? The arrogant fuck*. Marion must have let out a noise because all eyes turned to her.

Nonetheless, the detectives stood up, said their goodbyes and left.

Arthur was very pleased with himself at how calm he had remained during the conversation with the police.

After initially fearing that they had it all figured out and came to arrest him, he realized they didn't have a clue. And Arthur felt certain he hadn't given them any reason to be suspicious.

Arthur could see that Marion was devastated. It was not his intention to hurt her like this, but he never considered how her father's death, no…father's murder, would affect her. He obviously didn't care much at all. He sat next to Marion and extended his hand. Must be the concerned husband right now. Marion suddenly broke down in hysterical tears.

"I killed Daddy," Marion blurted through the tears.

Arthur couldn't believe his ears. "What?" he said astonished.

"I killed my father, that's what I said. Oh my god, that's what I DID!"

Arthur was beyond baffled. "Breathe, take a deep breath. Calm down and tell me what you're talking about."

Marion began reciting everything she remembered. "I was having a drink with Daddy at the bar. I was trying to convince him that Jankowski wasn't up to the task of running the company. He was rude and dismissive and then he said he thought it was the best thing for all of us. I lost it. I hit him over the head with a wine bottle. When he started to move I knew I had to finish the job. I went for the gun cabinet. We struggled and then I shot him. And I shot him again. There was a lot of blood and I left."

Arthur sat in disbelief and said, "Tell me everything, even the smallest detail."

Marion wasn't sure why he wanted all the details, but she wanted to tell someone. She wanted to get if off her chest, as if it could somehow assuage her guilt. Blow by blow, Marion recounted all the details of the murder including where she put the gun.

But, of course, they were not her memories, they were Arthur's, and that made no sense. For a brief moment Arthur thought Marion was playing some weird game with him, but this was a genuine confession. Detail after detail came out of her mouth identical to what actually happened.

"I don't know. When he said this really is the best thing for all of us, it just set me off." Marion continued, "Who knew I had the strength to knock him out?"

Arthur just took it all in, amazed at how things were unfolding.

After reliving the murder in retelling it to Arthur, Marion was exhausted. Arthur convinced her to take a sedative and lay down.

"I have to go to work," Arthur said calmly.

"No, I need you here," Marion said in a panic. "Besides you have a flat tire."

"How do you know I have a flat?" Arthur inquired.

"I saw it last night when I left for the big house. What? Now I'm calling it the big house too."

"I need to talk to the staff. Let them know." Arthur paused then added, "You just rest, and I'll be back before you know it."

Marion nodded and headed for bed.

Before Arthur left for work he felt it prudent to hide the gun in a location that Marion was unaware of. He hid it in the basement in the casing of an old time clock he had stolen from his first job. He had vowed never to have to punch a clock again. Oddly enough, the company decided to replace the time clock and had people fill out their own time cards instead. Arthur got his wish.

At work Arthur feigned shock and sadness over his boss' death, but the real fun was listening to the speculation of who the murderer was. When he could, Arthur would slip in something about the police always looking at who had the most to gain.

Jankowski had a very uncomfortable look on his face when Arthur mentioned that. But most of his colleagues concluded that Mrs. Carver would be the likely candidate as far as personal gain.

They might discard Mrs. Carver as a suspect if they knew the company was being left to Marion but that was not common knowledge. Few knew that Alice Carver was in the early stages of Alzheimer's and was not capable of managing the company.

It was especially interesting to watch Jankowski overplay his role. He wasn't fooling anyone, well, certainly not Arthur. He was ecstatic that the announcement of his succession to the throne had already been made. Surely he must know all that could change now, but he didn't let on. Arthur didn't challenge him on it either so as not to appear too eager. He knew the will would come to light soon enough.

Marion was asleep when Arthur arrived home. He sat down at the kitchen table with a freshly poured drink. There must be a logical answer to this magic of some sort. Clearly Marion had adopted his memories as her own. As impossible as it seemed, there was also something strangely familiar about it. It took a few minutes but finally he remembered. There was the time when Arthur was a boy and the neighbor kid stayed over. Arthur snuck downstairs and stole some money from his mother's purse. All night he worried about getting caught. However when the kid woke up, he was all panicky. He told Arthur he had stolen the money and rushed to put it back. Arthur figured the kid had seen him with the money and dreamt the rest.

Then there was the time his girlfriend in college took the blame for stealing the answers to their chemistry final. Somehow, some way he had imprinted his memories onto their subconscious minds. He wondered how that could be possible but there was a part of him that knew this was just something that was always there. Why look a gift horse in the mouth? This gift was his to use as he saw fit.

But if he were to use it again he would need to know how it works. He began searching for the common thread to all these instances. So it always occurred when Arthur had done something wrong and felt extremely guilty about it. However, that really didn't apply to this current case. He was, however, intensely worried about getting caught. Maybe that was it. Not guilt, but fear, or maybe all of the above.

Guilt, fear, intensity. Take those aspects to the extreme level and you have the common denominator. It worked once, it could work again...if need be.

Also, the other person would always wake up with the memories as if they had been planted there overnight. Arthur realized that he was just guessing at possibilities and that he needed to do research to nail this down. More like trial and error field work, he thought.

Chapter 5

It was early evening before Marion awoke. She was groggy but not so much that she didn't remember her situation. Arthur suggested they talk about their options, and Marion agreed.

"Okay, I've given this some thought," Arthur began. "Clearly the police haven't come to arrest you so there must not be any glaring evidence that points to you. We could call our lawyer and have him intervene, but I think that reeks of guilt." Marion started to interrupt but Arthur pressed on. "So I think we should keep this whole thing to ourselves. If the cops ask, I can be your alibi. I'll just say you were home with me the whole night."

Marion was touched by his support and willingness to lie for her. Still, her father had always preached that whenever any kind of legal issue arose, call your lawyer. Don't try and handle it yourself. She reminded Arthur of this but he resisted.

"I understand that approach in business matters and in some personal matters as well, but this is murder,

Marion. Need I remind you that our lawyer is also your mother's lawyer and a close friend of your father?" Arthur was adamant, "Lawyer, client privilege be damned. Do you really think he'll keep his mouth shut or even be working in your best interests?"

"We could get a different lawyer," Marion suggested. "One who specializes in criminal law."

"And how will that look? Avoid the family lawyer and get a criminal defense attorney when the police aren't even accusing you of anything? I'll tell you what it would look like...*GUILT!!!* Like you're hiding something and guess what...you are hiding something! A little thing called *MURDER*." Arthur lowered his voice and continued, "When they see you inherit the company and put me in charge, it spells motive. And a motive that involves both of us, so me being your alibi wouldn't mean a thing to them. You add motive to you getting a new lawyer and you might as well scream 'I did it!' to the world."

Arthur was pleased with his logic but completely unprepared for Marion's response. "What if I don't make you the head of the company? What if I leave Stan in charge? That would pretty much eliminate the motive and completely leave you out of it. I don't want you to get in trouble for something I've done."

Arthur felt like he was being told "it's really the best thing for everyone" all over again. It's a good thing there wasn't a wine bottle handy or he might have responded the same way he did when Carver said it.

"Don't be ridiculous. This is what we wanted from the start," Arthur said angrily.

"Yes, but not like this," said Marion. "This is not what I wanted!"

"Isn't it? Isn't that exactly what set us, uh…you, off? Isn't that why you killed him?"

"No!" Marion shouted. "That's not why!"

"Of course it is, Marion," Arthur insisted. "I know you didn't plan it. I know you didn't want to kill him but it doesn't change the fact that it was indeed the reason you did it."

Marion was quietly sobbing now as Arthur said in a calmer voice, "Listen, we both know I can run this company better than Jankowski. To let him take over would be a disservice to your father and all the hard work he put in to make the company the success that it is."

"But that's just it," Marion said resolutely. "It was *his* hard work and *his* decision to hand it over to Stan. The least I can do is honor his plan for the company's future."

Arthur was looking for a rebuttal, but his rage was making it hard to think.

"One more thing, honey," Marion added. "This removes all doubt as to who truly gains from Daddy's death."

"Dammit! Why shouldn't we gain from his death? We're his family." Arthur knew he had not chosen his words carefully, but he was too angry to walk it back. "Maybe you don't mind," Arthur emphasized. "It's not your career being trashed. You have your little girlfriend to run to. All I have is a shit marriage and a job with no future."

Marion was too stunned to respond. She was certain she had been discreet, but apparently not discreet enough.

Arthur pressed on, "If you don't have the decency to support my right to the company, and obviously you don't have the decency to adhere to our marriage vows, then maybe a divorce is in order." Arthur exhaled in relief that he had finally said it.

Marion was still taken aback by the revelation that Arthur knew of her affair. She barely heard him until he said "divorce." There is not a word in the English language that describes the feeling when your spouse shocks you with the first talk of divorce.

Arthur knew he had gone too far, primarily because divorce would destroy his chances of achieving his goal. Marion would inherit, keep Jankowski on and ask Arthur to resign. Something like *it would be best for everyone*, he imagined. But he was too angry to apologize and try to work it out right now. He needed to get away somewhere and think.

Arthur shook his finger at Marion and said, "Not now. I refuse to deal with you right now." Giving her a disgusted look, he grabbed his keys off the table and left.

Marion put her head down and cried.

Chapter 6

Sitting at the bar at his favorite pub, Arthur tried to sort things out. He had to come up with a plan, but Marion's insistence that Jankowski take over Carver Industries made things more complicated. Still, Arthur had confidence in his planning skills and was equally confident of his abilities to improvise if need be. After all, the original plan was just to talk to Martin, and he ended up killing the old coot. He followed that up with the plan to keep from getting caught and next thing you know, Marion believes she's the killer.   So   now he had to figure out how to get Marion to change her mind about Jankowski. Funny how his thoughts went straight to murder. It never used to be that way but if he could convince Marion that she killed her father then why not convince someone else that they killed Marion. Or should he kill Jankowski?

If he killed Jankowski would Marion still insist on giving the CEO job to someone else under the guise of protecting Arthur? If he killed Marion he might lose claim to the company to Alice Carver. Alice was more than happy to pass the company down to Marion, but she never liked Arthur and would surely fight for control of the company. Especially if her sister Jean had her way. So he would have to wait for all the legal paperwork to go through transferring the company to Marion before he could kill her. That could take weeks, maybe months. Any number of things could happen to muck up the works in that amount of time.

For now, he decided, he would focus on keeping Marion from being caught. And, like with Carver, he would try and convince her that he is the one for the job. If she agreed, then no further action would be needed. Arthur let out a barely audible chuckle as it dawned on him that he could use his gift to imprint the idea of him being appointed as CEO. The beauty in that is Marion will believe it was her own idea.

Earlier that day, Detectives Bailey and Schwartz decided they would make the two hour drive south to Cape Girardeau to inform Alice Carver of her husband's death. Although she was purportedly hours away at her sister's, spouses were almost always at the top of the suspect list in murder cases. Det. Gwen Bailey felt like she could get a better read on Mrs. Carver if she were there when she heard the news.

From the moment Det. Bailey met Mrs. Carver she all but dismissed her as a suspect. She was rather frail with an air of confusion about her. Mrs. Murdoch had warned them of her mother's condition and it became apparent within minutes. She understood what she was being told, but she made several references to her husband as if he were in the next room.

"I really should have my husband here. I don't know what I can tell you." Later she added, "My husband will know what to do."

Her sister Jean Honeycutt, however, understood completely and was eager to add her two cents. "That weasel of a son-in-law, I bet he did it. I wouldn't put it past him at all."

"Why would you say that Mrs. Honeycutt?" Schwartz asked politely.

"He always hated Martin. He pretended to like him but we, Alice and I, we could see right through his act. He married Marion for her money, of that there is no doubt." She raised her voice and continued, "I'm telling you, that's who you need to look at, that's who you need to arrest."

Alice was of little help to the detectives and Jean just kept rambling on about Arthur the weasel. She did, however, give Bailey and Schwartz good reason to take a look at Arthur's motive and alibi. They would talk to him tomorrow morning, but now they had to get back to St. Louis.

When they arrived at the station the preliminary police report was on Schwartz' desk. Danny Schwartz was surprised to read there were no signs of forced entry. He was certain it was a burglary gone wrong. However,

Bailey's instincts told her this was not a random murder. It made no sense that a burglar would leave all those guns just sitting there in an open cabinet. There had been a struggle, the broken glass on the cabinet door was proof of that. No, this was likely a crime of passion, a heated argument, a murder of opportunity. Hopefully the coroner's report would tell her more but it would not be complete for several days.

Just then Bailey was handed a note from a uniform cop. It appeared they received a phone call from a neighbor of their murder victim. The caller said she had seen something that might interest the police. Schwartz had already left for the day but Gwen decided she would stop on her way home and talk to this witness.

Celia Dawkins, the witness, was a talkative sort. She offered Gwen tea twice and discussed her dog's recent health issues before she uttered a word about the case.

"Ma'am, I was wondering if we could talk about what you saw," Det. Bailey urged.

"Oh yes, well, I was up rather late that night, my arthritis was making it difficult to clean up the dishes from supper. I know, I should have had them done hours before but I wanted to finish my book. It's the new one by..."

"Ma'am please," Gwen finally said.

"Oh yes, well, I was up late that night and I was in the kitchen when I saw the car go by. Not unusual but when you live in a cul-de-sac with only four houses, well, you notice things."

"I see. Do you know what time you saw this car?"

"Oh yes, it was 9:47," Mrs. Dawkins stated matter-of-factly.

"That's pretty exact on the time. You looked at the clock?" Gwen asked.

"Oh yes, it's right next to the kitchen window so I checked the time. Normally I'm in bed by nine but I was up late that night."

By now Bailey was fully aware of that fact. "Mrs. Dawkins, was the car coming in or going out of the street?"

"It was going that way," she said as she pointed her index finger to the left.

"Could you describe the car?" Gwen pressed.

"Oh no, I don't know anything about cars, but I don't need to. I know whose car it was."

Gwen waited for her to continue but it wasn't happening so she spoke, "You were saying ma'am, whose car was it?"

"Oh, it was the daughter's car. Marion's car. She's a good daughter, visits often." She sighed and continued, "Must be nice to have children who make time for their parents."

"Are you sure it was her car Mrs. Dawkins?"

"Oh yes, she visits often. I recognize her car...bright blue, easy to spot." Celia replied.

"Was Mrs. Murdoch driving?" Gwen inquired.

"Who, oh yes, that's Marion's married name, I forgot. Well I'm sure she was driving, it was her car," she looked at Gwen like she was stupid for not coming to the same conclusion.

A bit annoyed, there was an edge to her voice now. "But did you actually see Marion Murdoch driving the car?"

"Well I guess not. It was dark you know. My eyesight is good for my age but I can't see in the dark, young lady." She gave her that "are you stupid" look again.

Bailey quickly ascertained that she knew nothing more and went on her way. She contemplated a trip to the Murdoch home but decided it could wait till morning.

Chapter 7

Before Bailey could leave for the Murdoch's, Schwartz announced he had received a call from a Mr. Jankoski.

"So this Jankowski guy says that Marion Murdoch will inherit the company, not the wife." Schwartz paused, "Makes for a good motive, don't you think?"

"Yes I do, Danny boy, yes indeed," Gwen said smugly.

Schwartz went on, "He also poked a few jabs at Arthur Murdoch as well. He said," he paused as he read from his notes, "if Carver had been killed two weeks ago Arthur would have been handed the company by his wife, but since he, Jankowski, has been named as the successor, that wouldn't be the case now. Oh, called him a greedy little bastard too."

"Time to pay the Murdoch's a visit," Bailey said as she fumbled for her keys.

Not surprisingly it was another restless night for Marion and Arthur albeit for different reasons.

Despite Marion's plea for help in making funeral arrangements, Arthur cited pressing business affairs that he needed to resolve at work. So when Bailey and Schwartz arrived she was in a sleep deprived state all alone...just her and her guilt.

"Good morning, Mrs. Murdoch," Det. Schwartz said with a smile.

Marion was uneasy, "I don't feel well. Can you please come back tomorrow when my husband is home?" she begged.

Schwartz seemed almost willing to oblige but Bailey had been thinking all evening about the case and had no intention of leaving.

"Mrs. Murdoch, I know this is a difficult time, but we just have a few questions," Bailey began.

"I'm just not up to talking about it right now," Marion replied.

"Ma'am we are in the middle of a police investigation of a homicide and we..."

"Marion." Schwartz interrupted his partner and with a softer tone added, "It's just that finding out who murdered your father is a top priority for us, and I'm sure it is for you as well." Marion nodded slightly and Schwartz continued, "There's just a few things we need help with."

"Okay," that seemed like a reasonable request to Marion.

"The most obvious question we need to ask is why..."

Why I killed him, Marion thought, as her heart started to race.

"I'm sorry," Det. Bailey corrected herself, "I'm sorry, *who* might have a problem with your father? For instance, how are things with your parents' marriage? Any problems?"

"No!" Marion exclaimed. "My mother loves, loved my father and he loved her. She would never hurt him."

"Well I understand she is ill. Did that put additional strain on the marriage?"

"I told you, he took wonderful care of her. Besides, she's in the early stages, most of the time she's her old self. She just forgets things on occasion." Marion was clearly upset.

"It's okay Mrs. Murdoch, we're just trying to get a good picture of the situation." Schwartz interjected with his "good cop" voice.

Det. Bailey didn't think for a minute Mrs. Carver was the killer, but it got Marion Murdoch on the defensive. It has been her experience that when suspects get defensive they either scream for their lawyer or they let something slip. This was a risk she was willing to take. After finishing her queries about Alice Carver she got to the point.

"Where were you last Sunday night, Mrs. Murdoch?"

Marion felt her jaw drop. "I was here all day, all night, never left the house."

"Alone?"

"No, Arthur was here with me."

"Was that before or after you went to your father's house?" Bailey said flatly.

"What are you talking about it?" Marion stuttered.

"We spoke with Mrs. Dawkins, and she saw you leaving."

"She saw me?" Marion was tripping over her words now, "I mean she said that, not like, she really saw me or something. What time did she see me? Uh, you know what I mean." Marion tried to cover her slip of the tongue with a chuckle but Bailey wasn't buying it.

"What difference does it make if you were never there, Mrs. Murdoch?" Bailey was pushing now.

"None of course, how silly. No Celia must be mistaken. We were home all day." Marion paused then added, "Perhaps I should call my lawyer."

"We just have a few more questions then we'll be on our way," Det. Schwartz joined in. "Perhaps your husband went to see your father. I understand they had a difficult relationship. Maybe some problem at work?"

Bailey was furious that Danny had diverted the conversation away from Mrs. Murdoch, but Schwartz continued before she could stop him. "Maybe there was an argument, maybe it turned violent. Is your husband a violent man, Marion?"

"No! My husband is not a violent man! My husband did not kill daddy! I killed him! I did it! I was just so angry. I don't know what came over me. I just don't know what came over me."

Both Bailey and Schwartz were more than a bit stunned by the sudden confession.

Chapter 8

Once again Arthur was forced to improvise his company coup. There was no avoiding getting the lawyer involved now. Time for plan B.

It was hours before Arthur was allowed to see his wife. In the interim he decided his next move. "How are you honey?" Arthur said in a seemingly genuine way.

Marion fought back tears as she discussed her meeting with the lawyer. "I told him not to bother defending me but he begged me to reconsider. I feel the right thing is to accept my punishment. God knows I deserve it." Marion was resolute.

It took some work but Arthur persuaded Marion to accept the lawyer's help. A graphic description of a lifetime in prison did the trick.

Arthur put his hand on the glass that separated them. She reciprocated as if to press her palm against his. Speaking through the phone that connected them, he softly said, "Just know this. We will fight this together. I love you. You don't have to go through this alone."

Marion was moved by his unexpected affection and support. "I love you, too."

"I'm sorry. I only said that bit about divorce because I was hurt. You cheated on me and then you told me I wasn't good enough to run your father's company."

"I'm sorry too, Arthur. I'm sorry about the affair. I never meant to hurt you, I was so lonely. You never seemed to be around. You were always working or something." Tears were rolling down her cheeks.

"I was doing it for us, for our future. And how do you repay me? You take a lover AND the company...now you want to give it all away." Arthur hung his head to give the appearance of being deeply hurt.

"I'm sorry, baby, really sorry. It's over. I ended the affair. It won't happen again." Then Marion looked puzzled and asked, "How did you know?"

Arthur decided to go with a vague answer instead of the truth. There was no need to tell her he followed her from time to time. "I just knew."

"You just knew I was having an affair with a woman?" Marian doubted he was that intuitive.

"Well, I saw you with her once, a while back at a restaurant. It was pretty obvious what was going on."

"What restaurant? Oh never mind, it doesn't matter now. I ended the affair weeks ago." Marion looked lovingly at Arthur, "It's only us now, sweetheart, only us."

Arthur knew she was lying, it was less than a week, and he couldn't care less. Regardless, he mimicked a kiss, smiled, and replied, "That's right honey, you and me always. And I'll forgive the affair if you forgive me for neglecting you." On the inside Arthur was choking on those words. He had nothing to be forgiven for.

When he left the county jail, he headed straight to work. Immediately after arriving, Jankowski called Arthur into his office. "How's your wife Art?" Jankowski asked.

Like you care is what Arthur wanted to say, but he resisted. "As well as she can be, but it's difficult to lose a father and then be falsely accused of his murder."

Jankowski looked confused. "I thought she confessed."

"No, that's a lie!" Arthur said firmly. When in doubt, deny, deny, deny was Arthur's philosophy. "Where did you hear that anyway?"

"It was in the news."

"Well, it's a lie. She didn't confess, and she didn't kill Martin!"

Moving on Jankowski said, "I didn't expect to see you back so soon. I assumed you needed some time off."

"I need to work. Besides, I figured with Mr. Carver gone, you could use some help with the transition. Well, I guess transition isn't the right word anymore. You're the boss, and I'm here to help in any way I can."

"I appreciate that, Art." Jankowski didn't believe Arthur for a second. However, he was the boss now and it didn't really matter whether Arthur supported him or not.

Arthur left the office secure in the belief he could maneuver himself into the number two man in the company. Then if anything tragic should befall Jankowski...Arthur smiled a wicked grin.

Chapter 9

As difficult as it was, Arthur spent the next few weeks making himself invaluable to Jankowski and pledging his devotion to Marion. Her lawyer, Jackson Brooks, managed to get a hearing scheduled to dispute the legality of Marion's confession. Marion told her attorney she had requested a lawyer during the initial interview and that she had made the request prior to her confession.

In court, Det. Bailey testified the mention of a lawyer was not in the form of a request. However, Det. Schwartz told the judge it could have been perceived as a request for an attorney.

The judge ruled in Marion's favor, saying the confession had been illegally obtained. Once the confession was tossed, Marion's attorney was able to get bail set, albeit a huge amount, one million dollars. As much as Arthur enjoyed his time alone, he needed her out of jail. Only then could he convince her to remove Jankowski and have Arthur take his place. Fortunately, for Arthur, Alice Carver put up the bail.

Arthur picked up his wife from the jail just before five. After taking her home to clean up, they went to her favorite restaurant to celebrate. The evening concluded with some really enthusiastic sex. Arthur thought, had he known this would be the result of her getting out of jail, he'd have sent her there sooner.

After she fell asleep, Arthur got started. While lying next to her he thought long and hard about Marion naming him as the new CEO. He planted doubts in Marion's mind about Jankowski's competence. He focused on how happy Marion was with her decision to turn the company over to Arthur. He instilled some guilt about not having done this in the first place. Arthur did all those things while digging deep to tap into his own fear of failure. Guilt and fear, these were the ingredients for a successful imprint.

Arthur sat patiently throughout breakfast waiting for Marion to talk about the future of the company now that Arthur was running it. Growing weary of this wait, Arthur broached the subject. "I was thinking a lot last night about the direction the company should take now that I'm in charge."

"In charge? What are you talking about? C'mon, we discussed this. It's kind of funny that you mention this. I had a dream last night that I gave you the company. In my dream, I felt a little guilty about the whole thing. I think the whole point of the dream was to remind me why I put Jankowski in charge. It's for the best."

"Are you fucking kidding me? For the best?" Arthur shouted.

"Oh god, I'm sorry, poor choice of words. It's just, well, now that the confession's been thrown out, the detectives will be looking for other evidence to put me away. Like I said, how would it look if I suddenly replaced Jankowski with my husband?"

"You've made a big mistake, a big mistake!" Arthur said in a threatening tone. However, the mistake was his. He could see he had frightened Marion which did not bode well for the success of his plan. Of course, the imprint didn't work so his plan was already in peril.

Arthur took a long way to work trying to figure out why the imprint failed. It was all about the common denominators of fear, guilt and intensity. It boiled down to the fact, Plan B had hit a snag. Now what? Arthur thought. Plan C, plan D, plan E, F, G? Arthur decided the plans were the problem. They had been passive and manipulative, and they had failed.

Only when the fear had been real, only when the intensity had been extreme, that's when it worked. And like the plan, the imprint attempt last night had been passive. It was time to get aggressive. He felt confident, if done correctly, the imprint could work again.

And what could be more intense and extreme than murder? With Jankowski gone, Marion would have to see things his way.

Chapter 10

Arthur spent the next few days digging into the life of Stan Jankowski. For Arthur, there must be two victims of a murder. One dead and one to take the blame. He had clearly decided on the murder victim, now he had to find a patsy. Unfortunately, Arthur was not a private detective. He had no clue how to uncover any dirt. Marion had once told him, "If you want to know the personal stuff about a man...don't ask his wife, ask his secretary."

Arthur wasn't good at casual conversation, but he was making an attempt with Stan Jankowski's executive secretary, Ashley.

One such attempt yielded exactly what he was looking for.

"Stan working late tonight, I see." Arthur shook his head in mild disapproval and smiled.

"At least he's actually here," Ashley replied.

"What do you mean, Ashley?" Arthur was indeed curious.

"It's just, well, sometimes when he leaves he says 'if my wife calls, tell her I'm in a meeting.' Then I'm supposed to text him and let him know she called. I really don't like lying to his wife," Ashley said in a low voice.

"Where does he go?" Arthur intentionally sounded naive.

Ashley hesitated, "Oh, I don't know, it's probably nothing." She paused again and added in a whisper, "He does like his martinis." She made the gesture of tipping an imaginary glass to her lips.

Arthur nodded and went on his way. He then waited in his car around the corner where he could see the exit from the parking garage. When he spotted Jankowski's car leaving, he followed.

For the first time Arthur felt in complete control of his own fate. Killing Carver was the chaotic result of poor planning and indecisiveness. There was no true commitment on Arthur's part, he left too much to chance. This time he was all in and it was exhilarating. The rush of excitement combined with the intensity of his focus was almost more than he could bear. He wondered if this is what cold blooded killers felt leading up to the kill. Is this what drives them to kill again and again? With evil delight Arthur smiled realizing HE was about to be the cold blooded killer he was just now wondering about.

Engulfed in euphoria, Arthur nearly missed Jankowski turning at the light. Following someone undetected was part of the thrill, knowing that Stan was completely unaware that his killer was just a few car lengths behind him.

Ultimately, an unsuspecting Stan Jankowski was setting the stage for his own demise. A momentary flash of fear startled Arthur, *What if this stalking yielded nothing?* It's possible Stan was just heading to a bar to get tanked. This was the only lead Arthur had, there was no backup plan.

Just then Stan turned down Cherokee Street. During the day this was a street lined with cafes and antique shops but by night this was the stroll. In front of the closed storefronts were prostitutes displaying their wares and the men who drove up to procure their services. Arthur was certain that Stan did not have antique shopping on his mind.

Arthur slammed on his brakes a little too hard. He had stayed back a few cars to avoid detection, but suddenly Stan was passing him going in the opposite direction. Fortunately, Stan was too busy cruising the hookers to notice Arthur just ten feet away. As inconspicuously as possible, Arthur moved on and made a quick U-turn at the end of the block. In doing so, he was now directly behind Stan. Certainly a TV cop show is no guide to a murder but he had thought it taught him better about how to follow a car. Arthur hung back and slunk down in his seat. This was just a two lane road and the business taking place, being what it is, made it typical for the traffic to move extremely slow. Rarely did anyone try to pass. Men were all there for the same thing, except for the occasional group of teenagers howling a variety of unpleasantries at the girls.

Stan came to a halt as he pulled over to the curb. There was room for Arthur to pass but there was no one behind him so he just stopped too. Obviously Arthur knew what was happening, still he was a bit surprised when a young man, barely old enough to not be a boy, climbed into Stan's car.

Busy watching Stan, Arthur didn't notice the woman who had walked up to his passenger side window. As she leaned in to talk to him, he dismissed her and jolted forward before she could remove her hands from the car door. He glanced in his rear view and saw that she had been knocked down. Needless to say, Arthur could not have cared less.

With just a couple of short turns, Stan pulled up to a surprisingly nice motel that didn't look the part of a hooker motel. Arthur continued down the block, turned around, turned off his lights and parked on the street with the motel still in view.

Well, this was it, Arthur thought, *this was the dirt he was looking for.* He hadn't worked out the details but already a plan was formulating in his head.

Stan went into the motel office while the kid stayed in the car. It appeared that Stan didn't want anyone seeing the kid as he was slumped in his seat hiding behind the dashboard. A couple of minutes later Stan came out and drove just a few parking spaces down the lot. Stan looked around like he was trying to sneak into the room undetected. Arthur thought this was particularly silly since no one he knew would possibly be there unless they were with a pro as well. Of course, there was someone watching Stan and it would be the death of him.

Uncertain as to what to do next, Arthur just waited. The kid left a half hour later and started walking instead of getting into Stan's car. Arthur decided to follow him. After all, there are two victims in Arthur's murder plot. When the kid was nearly out of sight, Arthur got out of his car and continued on foot. Less than two blocks later the kid entered an old two family flat. Arthur wasn't sure if this was his apartment or another customer but before he could think of his next move, the kid came out of the building and headed back the way he came.

Arthur waited a minute then walked up to the door. The apartment was dark and Arthur boldly knocked on the door. There was no answer. Arthur got back in his car to head home, with one slight detour. On one last pass on the stroll, he spotted the kid. He was back on his corner, hustling, just like Arthur had hoped.

Arthur decided to alter his route to drive by the motel and was pleasantly surprised to see Stan's car still in the lot. Perfect, Arthur thought, just perfect.

Chapter 11

It had been months since Vic went to the bar with hooking up on her mind. Marion had fulfilled that need admirably. But now Marion was out of the picture and the old tried and true method was back on the menu. Her method was simple. Peruse the bar for a woman on her own and charm the pants off her, quite literally. The tricky part was weeding out the ones looking for the magic of true love.

Vic didn't believe in love. It was messy, boring, annoying and sometimes, when she least expected it, painful. She much preferred hot, passionate sex without the strings. Even if the sex turned into a relationship of sorts, the expectations were minimal. Only when you fell into the state of "coupledom" did she find herself trapped in a world full of "feelings" and compromise. Vic found few things as boring and annoying than situations like choosing what movie to watch on a Friday night. It's like an awkward dance between being selfish or being submissive. Vic thought the latter, submissive, was the worst when both parties took that approach. "What do you want to watch?" "Oh, whatever. What do YOU want to watch?" "I asked you first, sweetie" Etc. The excessive syrupy sweetness made Vic nauseous. She had been there before, and she wasn't going back.

"Hey stranger."

Vic felt a familiar hand on her shoulder to match the familiar voice. Vic turned to gaze into the living proof of just how painful love can be. Once again Vic found herself pulling away from Janey, when in fact she wanted only to draw her close and hold her tight.

"How've you been?" Vic astonished herself. *Wow, what a lame response* she thought. She wondered why all her charm and confidence went right out the window when she talked with Janey.

"I've been good. Work is crazy. Speaking of crazy, how's your world?" Janey replied.

That might have offended someone else but Vic knew she deserved it. She had put Janey thru hell when they were together. And how was Janey rewarded for her tolerance and patience? With an abrupt disappearing act. Vic just stopped coming home, a home she and Janey shared. Then after a week she came home while Janey was at work and unceremoniously packed up all her things and left.

Vic had the internal discussion many times about why she left. Not surprisingly there was a scenario about what movie they would watch one Friday night. When the passion dwindles so does the relationship, or so Vic says she believes. And yet the discussion in her head repeats itself frequently in an obvious attempt to convince herself that love is messy, boring and annoying.

"Have a drink with me, J?" Vic asked *but why would you?* is what she thought. *Why would anyone for that matter?* Vic thought. *This is what love does to you. This is what Janey does to you.* And yet Vic desperately wanted Janey to say yes.

Not wanting to be alone with Vic, Janey replied, "Come join us, we've got a table."

"Some other time", Vic smiled and gave Janey a sincere look that said, maybe, just maybe, I'll be able to be around you again someday.

Janey knew she was not being dismissed. She gently held Vic's hand, smiled warmly and said, "Soon I hope, Vic, soon."

Vic lost interest in her sexual pursuit after her encounter with Janey. She flirted haphazardly with the bartender, but her heart wasn't in it. She was about to leave when she felt a compelling urge to be responsible. Clearly she had too much to drink, clearly Janey was watching her, and clearly the bartender would not be impressed by some drunk getting behind the wheel. So that all would notice, Vic pretended to have forgotten her phone and asked the cute little bartender with too many tattoos to call her a cab. The bartender nodded approvingly and made the call.

Chapter 12

Arthur cruised through the next week, not letting Marion or Stan unnerve him. Everything was ready for Friday night. He was even mentally prepared for the possibility that Friday night might not be the night. He felt certain he had convinced Marion of his sincerity in his effort to be Stan's right hand man. Besides she had her legal issues to deal with. Arthur felt confident that Marion would still end up in prison, but, if all went according to plan, he would be so entrenched in the CEO position that the outcome of Marion's trial would be irrelevant.

Working closely with Stan made it easy to follow his schedule. Friday night came and Stan worked till just after 8. Meanwhile, Arthur left at 7:30 and hung out in the parking lot across the street. He pretended to be on the phone in case anyone noticed him. He awkwardly changed his clothes to impersonate a teenager. He had bought a pair of long, baggy shorts like he saw the kid wearing. The sleeveless tee, which Arthur's generation not so lovingly called a "wife beater" was under his easily removed dress shirt. And the hoodie was just to hide the obvious middle-aged man underneath his youthful wardrobe.

As soon as Arthur saw Stan exit the office, he started his car. It quickly became apparent that Stan was heading for his Cherokee Street cruise. Following him this time was so much easier, already knowing his destination.

As Stan slowly rolled down the street, Arthur's heart began to race. He knew now what people meant when they said they never felt more alive. Arthur patted the cloth bag on the passenger seat as a reassurance that he had everything he needed for the night's festivities. Arthur spotted the kid and clearly Stan did as well. Once again, the kid got into Stan's car as they drove the three blocks to the motel.

As Stan pulled into the motel lot, Arthur drew a deep breath and steeled himself for the kill. His focus was intense and his senses heightened. He grabbed the gloves out of the bag and put them on. He rehearsed his lines one last time. It was crucial he got them right.

After a few minutes Stan stepped out of the motel office and walked down to Room 108. The kid waited in the parking lot, out of sight from the office door. A couple of minutes after Stan entered the room the kid knocked and Stan let him in.

Arthur waited patiently with a clear view of the room. He felt amazingly calm. The thrill of his stalking and planning was now a calm resolve.

When the kid came out, Arthur was ready. He waited

till the kid was out of sight, presumably walking back to the stroll.

Arthur got out of his car and tucked the sheath with the hunting knife into his waistband behind his back. One last deep breath and Arthur knocked on the door of Room 108.

As Stan opened the door he spoke, "Did you forget...?" His voice trailed off and he froze.

"Hello Stanley."

"What are *you* doing here?" Stan was visibly nervous.

"We need to talk," Arthur said firmly.

"What the hell do you want?" There was fear and anger in Stan's voice.

"Let me in now unless you want us to have it out in front of the whole world."

"Get inside," Stan said reluctantly.

Arthur stepped in and squared up to Stan with just a couple of feet separating them. "I think maybe I want a little more than my usual fee. The missus would be none too pleased with what we do here. How much is my silence worth to you?"

"What *we* do?" Stan looked puzzled. "What are you talking about? Blackmail? Is that what we're talking about here?"

"Call it what you want."

"You've got some nerve, Art. You could find yourself out on the street in a heartbeat."

Arthur winced at Stan using his name. "That's a funny thing to threaten me with."

"I have no problem calling the police. I'm sure they are quite familiar with you by now."

That was Arthur's cue and he acted quickly. Arthur pulled on the hunting knife, yanking it out if its sheath. Then, before Stan could react, Arthur plunged the knife full throttle into Stan's stomach. Stan's face turned ghostly white. It was the desperate look of a man who knew his life had just ended. Stan dropped to the floor without muttering a sound. Arthur reached down and removed the knife. For no apparent reason Arthur stomped on Stan's head several times. He bent over and checked Stan's pulse. His work was done.

Arthur was covered with more blood than he anticipated but that wasn't a bad thing. The hoodie was dark and covered up the red blood splashed all over the bright white undershirt.

Arthur left the motel seemingly unnoticed. He parked the car on a deserted street and changed back into his suit. He put the bloody clothes in a garbage bag he brought with him.

Immediately after doing so, he noticed blood on the steering wheel. Then he saw blood on the gearshift, the headrest and a small stain on the seat. The muscles in his neck and shoulders tightened. His head pounded. This was the first time tonight he was aware of any tension in his body. Taking a human life did not affect Arthur's calm, and he was determined not to let a little blood rattle him. He quickly wiped the blood covered areas and all but the smear on the seat were eradicated. *Another problem for another day*, Arthur thought.

Arthur did a quick drive by where the kid worked before heading over to the kid's apartment. Arthur parked in the alley behind the flat where it was sufficiently dark enough to keep him well hidden. He reached around to grab a small step ladder from the back seat, then grabbed the garbage bag with the bloody clothes and knife. He had noticed the last time he was here the bathroom window was kept partially open, and fortunately it was again. It wasn't a big window but it was big enough for Arthur to shimmy through. Once Arthur was inside, he reached back out the window and pushed the ladder over inthe tall grass, out of sight. Then he took his position under the bed along with the garbage bag... and waited.

He laid there in silence reviewing the events of the evening. He organized them in a way he would focus on during the imprint. He weeded out the part where Stan mentioned his name, but he feared it could surface in the process. The kid may question the memory if it included someone calling him Art.

That was the biggest unknown. Arthur was unsure how much he could control the flow of his complete memories and the selected ones he wished to imprint on his victims. Arthur focused on his breathing to remain perfectly still. It might be hours before the kid got home and remaining centered and calm was essential through all elements of the murder and imprint.

Suddenly his phone rang. His calm instantaneously changed to panic. He couldn't believe he so stupidly failed to mute his phone. He fumbled around frantically till he found his phone and turned it off. Arthur turned his attention to bringing his body and mind back to a peaceful state.

Several hours later Arthur heard the key turn in the front door lock, followed by footsteps, presumably the kid's. Arthur was keenly awake. The bed was shoved up against the far wall and Arthur was snuggled up against the wall. The kid watched a little television and puttered around in the kitchen a bit. Arthur could not control his nervousness. He was completely vulnerable. One glance under the bed and he would be completely exposed, in no position to do a damn thing. He tried not to think about it and focused on the task at hand. Just then the lights went out and Arthur could feel the sink of the mattress as the kid flopped down on the bed. Continuing to wait, Arthur stopped focusing on his own breathing and focused on the kid's instead. There was no way to be sure, but as the kid's breathing became slow and steady, Arthur surmised he was asleep.

Arthur began. *I walked up to the door of Room 108. "What are you doing here?" "We need to talk."* Start to finish. Every word, words specifically designed by Arthur to sound like he was the kid. Keeping in rhythm with his breathing for maximum focus. *I inserted the knife.* Exhale. *I stomped on his head.* Exhale. *I left the motel room.* Exhale. He started to follow that thought with going to his car but he quickly ended that thought and started over from the beginning. *I knocked on the door of Room 108...*

Arthur continued the process for about an hour. He feared much longer would be too risky. Arthur scuffled out from under the bed as quietly as he could. He crawled a few feet before standing up. Just as he stood, he heard a groan. The kid rolled over and Arthur darted around the corner into the living room.

With his back flush against the wall, he stayed out of view. Then he heard the kid get out of bed.

Arthur was not prepared for this scenario at all and was angry with himself for having been so shortsighted. He had no means of defending himself if he was discovered. He looked around for something he could use as a weapon. There was a heavy glass ashtray on the end table. It was a poor excuse for a weapon but it would have to suffice. He grabbed the ashtray and readied himself for a fight. Just then he heard the toilet flush. Arthur sighed in relief but did not let his guard down. He stood frozen as he listened to the kid get back into bed.

Arthur was afraid to move but even more afraid to stay. He waited a few minutes then decided it would be quicker to walk out the front door rather than climb back out the window. He crossed the room and opened the door with minimal creaking. If the kid woke up now, he could just run like hell. But the kid didn't wake up, and Arthur closed the door quietly behind him.

Then he went around back and picked up the ladder

and threw it in the back seat. Taking off his gloves, he stuffed them in the glove box and drove away.

On the way home Arthur relived every glorious moment of the night. He felt incredible. Nothing he had ever done in his entire life could measure up to this level of euphoria. As he replayed the night in his head, he chuckled out loud and realized this was just like the imprint process. If he kept this up he might end up convincing Marion that she killed Stan too. As funny as that sounded, he knew it would muck things up so he put an end to his reminiscing. Arthur knew he would have to clear his mind before crawling into bed with his wife. But he could do anything he set his mind to at this point. He had a lock on self-control and he knew he could shut off specific thoughts easily.

Arthur arrived home and slipped into the house. He climbed into bed next to his sleeping wife and cleared his mind just as he had instructed himself to do. Sleep came easily.

Marion kept her eyes closed and said nothing, but she was keenly aware that it was nearly dawn and her husband just came home.

Arthur awoke with a start. In a moment of self-doubt he feared there would be sirens and a multitude of cops rushing his front door. There weren't and with good reason, Arthur thought. He had left no reason for the cops to come calling. He turned on the TV to see if Stan's murder had made the morning news. It had not.

Marion puttered around the kitchen making little

huffing and sighing noises. Arthur knew it was bait for him to ask what's wrong but he wasn't biting.

Tired of waiting for the question, Marion spoke. "You were out late last night." She didn't want to let on that she knew exactly how late. "Seemed rather late for you to be working. I finally gave up and went to bed." She paused, "Well, were you working?"

"No," Arthur said abruptly.

Marion waited for him to continue but he didn't so she went ahead, "So where were you?"

"Not that it's any of your business, but I stopped and had a few drinks. Then I grabbed a bite at that diner near work."

"No need to be snippy about it. A phone call would have been nice. I was worried."

Exasperated, Arthur let out a perfunctory sorry, finished his coffee, and walked out the door.

Marion felt certain that Arthur was lying, but the thought of what he might actually have done was more than she cared to think about.

Chapter 13

Detectives Bailey and Schwartz were also sipping their morning joe. They were quietly doing paperwork when Gwen Bailey's phone rang.

"Homicide, Bailey," she answered.

"Hey, this is Espinosa in the liaison office. We've got a vic in the city you might be interested in. Uh, name of Stanley Jankowski." The city and county liaison office was designed to cross reference each other's database when a major crime occurs.

"Doesn't ring a bell," Bailey stated. "Why do you think it's of interest to us?"

"Well, I ran the name thru the system and it popped up in your notes on a homicide."

Bailey waited but nothing so she asked the obvious question, "What homicide are we talking about?"

"Martin Carver," Espinoza replied.

That definitely rang a bell with Bailey. She was immediately reminded of how they had gotten a confession from the daughter but the damn lawyer got it thrown out. More than once Bailey wondered why she bothered to do her job when the lawyers would just twist the facts until the whole case imploded.

"Yeah, I remember now. What's the scoop on the Jankowski homicide?" Bailey inquired.

"Looks like a simple case of a John getting himself killed by a hooker or, at least, that's the working theory. It's in the system if you want to check out the file. Case no SJ59146."

"Thanks Carlos, I'll do that." Bailey leaned forward on her desk. "So here's an interesting development, Danny." Bailey shared the new information with her partner.

"Think it's related?" Danny asked.

"Doesn't initially sound like it but I don't believe much in coincidence when it comes to homicide. Why don't you pull the paper copies of our notes on Carver and I'll print out the Jankowski file."

Danny shook his head at Bailey's obsession with paper copies as opposed to just reading the file on the computer. But that was just how she worked, and Danny respected her process.

Bailey grabbed the printout and started reading the case file.

Jankowski was found dead at the Beaumont hotel at 5:40 a.m. by the night manager, Norman Yates. He had multiple stab wounds to the stomach and chest and contusions to the face and skull. Jankowski was a regular at the motel, usually on Friday nights. There was a young man with him that Yates identified only as "Brick." He had been Jankowski's standing "date" for quite some time. Currently there was no legal name available for "Brick." Victim's immediate family has been notified. Lead detectives for the case: James Smith and Christina Harden.

Bailey exchanged files with Schwartz and began reviewing their notes on the Carver case. It didn't take a genius to see the obvious connection. Carver, CEO of Carver Industries...murdered. Jankowski, newly appointed CEO of Carver Industries...murdered. Who was next in line was the obvious question but Bailey felt certain she knew who it was, Arthur Murdoch, husband to their killer, Marion Murdoch.

Did Marion Murdoch also kill Jankowski? But if she wanted her husband to run the family business she already had that opportunity. Then there's the husband. He's the obvious beneficiary to the company throne. Then again, Occams Razor may apply. "When you have two competing theories, the simpler one is better," roughly translated. In other words, maybe this "Brick" kid did kill his john.

Danny chimed in with another possibility. "I never thought Marion Murdoch had the stones to kill her father and we never found the murder weapon. What if she hired someone? She had the money and now she's inherited more."

Bailey was impressed, which Schwartz was rarely able to do. "I'm gonna give Christina Harden a call. She's the lead in this new case, maybe she can shed some light."

Det. Harden did indeed have some new information that she willingly shared with Bailey. It didn't take long to identify "Brick" as Joey Brickell. The clerk at the liquor store, by the corner where Brick worked, knew exactly who he was as he cashed checks for him regularly. A couple of soliciting charges put him in the system with a current address. They easily got a warrant as this kid was a nobody and the criminal justice system provides little protection for nobodies. The search yielded a bag of bloody clothes and the apparent murder weapon, a hunting knife.

There were still a few details to work out before they could put this one to bed but Harden was confident they had the right guy.

Bailey knew Harden was a good detective but she found it hard to accept their conclusion in this case. The coincidence was too far-fetched. She knew she couldn't actively investigate the Jankowski murder but she could easily justify reopening the Carver case.

Chapter 14

Summer turned to fall and Arthur was starting to settle in at work. However at home his marriage was unraveling. Marion had officially been indicted and the trial was on the docket. Arthur had completely lost interest in his wife's upcoming trial and she knew it. For that matter, Arthur had completely lost interest in his wife entirely. She knew that, too.

What Arthur unexpectedly found was being unsatisfied with his current overall situation. He had the CEO job. He had gotten away with two murders. His marriage was not a happy one but it hadn't been for a long time. Surely he thought this would be enough. Surely it was not.

Marion sat staring out her kitchen window contemplating the meaning of life. Well, maybe just a meaning of her life. The trial was upon her and she felt lost and hopeless. The undying support her husband promised was clearly a lie. Her father was dead, by her hand. Her mother hated her, when she was in her right mind. Marion visited her occasionally but she never knew what kind of welcome she would get.

She needed someone. There was only one person she felt knew her and cared about her. She grabbed her phone and dialed Vic's number. When she didn't pick up Marion fumbled for words to leave on her voicemail. "I need to see you," and   "I miss you" were the essence of her rambling message.

Vic saw the caller ID and decided not to answer. She had work to keep her busy enough. Payroll was due. Quarterly taxes needed to be filed. Vic worked in the accounting office of a midsize graphics design firm. It wasn't a great job, but it paid the rent. She contemplated going back to school every now and then to get her degree, but that's as far as she would get.

Vic listen to Marion's message and knew what it meant. She had a decision to make. Go back to a friends-with-benefits relationship or continue the life of celibacy she had recently condemned herself to. Ever since she ran into Janey she had lost interest in one night stands. She viewed the relationship with Marion as a kind of middle ground. More than a hookup, less than a committed, monogamous relationship. She decided to return her call and meet up. If Marion started talking of love, Vic was hitting the pavement.

Det. Bailey felt like she was hitting a brick wall. She reinterviewed every single person associated with the Carver case and came up short of linking it to the

Jankowski murder. She convinced a judge to issue a new expanded warrant to search the Murdoch house again but did not find the murder weapon. On top of that, the evidence against Marion Murdoch was minimal, and there was a very good chance she would be acquitted.

All they had was the neighbor witnessing the car and traffic cameras confirming her account, but neither had a good view of the driver. Her fingerprints were all over the victim's home, including the gun cabinet, but it was her family's home so it was not surprising. There was no murder weapon which was puzzling as Mrs. Murdoch had clearly told them where it was.

And then there's the confession which was tossed out. Being the beneficiary of all that money could sway the jury but has no evidentiary value. If Carver hadn't been a major figure in the community, Bailey doubted there would even be a trial. Of course, Bailey had doubts about the entire case anyway.

The trial for the Jankowski murder was only a week away and a conviction seemed like a forgone conclusion. Once that happened there would be little chance that anyone would bother to look at the case again. Even if her instinct told her both cases were all wrong, there was nothing she could do about it. Bailey did not like resigning herself one bit to a resolution that she didn't for a second believe was the truth.

Chapter 15

Marion and Vic met up at Vic's favorite cafe in the Central West End. This was also adjacent to the Chase Park Plaza Hotel that they frequently retired to after lunch and drinks. It was an upscale hotel that Marion gladly paid for.

After they both sat down, Marion jumped right in, "I miss you." Vic was not going to get caught up in a conversation that could end up bringing up love, so she stayed silent.

"I know you're probably angry with me, but you hurt me and..." Marion stopped herself, "Nevermind that's the past. I understand where you're coming from."

Vic doubted that Marion had a clue where Vic was coming from. She decided on a relatively neutral statement, "I miss what we had."

That was enough for Marion. She smiled and touched Vic's hand. Seeing as how Marion generally shied away from public displays of affection, Vic was leery of where things were going. Still, she returned the gesture and decided to go with the moment. The moment became a pleasant lunch followed by a satisfying afternoon at the Chase Park Plaza Hotel.

Marion was visibly chipper when Arthur got home, and he found it quite suspicious.

"What are you so happy about? Did your lawyer call and say the key witness dropped dead?" Arthur smirked.

That was a low blow, even for Arthur, but Marion decided to let it slide. "No, I just had a lovely afternoon with a friend."

That sounded a bit off to Arthur but it was not worth his time. He shuffled off to the master bedroom to change his clothes.

Over the course of the next few days Marion had several "lovely afternoon with friends." Arthur went from annoyed, to curious, to suspicious. It sounded like another affair was happening and that pushed Arthur right from curious to furious. If he was forced to bear this intolerable marriage, sure as hell, she was too.

Arthur was too busy to spy on Marion himself so he hired a private detective. He had good reason to do so, and it might turn up some useful information he could use later.

Just when Gwen Bailey was learning to live with the travesty of the Jankowski and Carver cases she received a phone call from none other than Marion Murdoch.

"Mrs. Murdoch, I must say I'm surprised to hear from you."

"Well, I imagine so, but I was wondering if you could help me with something."

Like recording a new confession, Bailey thought. "That depends on what you need."

"I was wondering about Stan's murder, Stan Jankowski."

"Ma'am I can't really discuss a case with you."

"I understand but I just wondered if you were really certain that boy is the one who did it."

"Like I said ma'am, I can't discuss a case with you. Do you have any reason to believe otherwise? Or any information that indicates someone else as the perp, I mean, suspect?" Bailey's interest was piqued.

"No, I just, I guess I was just disturbed so much by what happened that I wanted to make sure you caught the right man."

"You sure there isn't something you want to tell me?" Bailey pressed. "Something you want to get off your chest?" It was a poor attempt to solicit another confession but she was put on the spot. It didn't work and they concluded their conversation.

Bailey wasn't sure what her options were, but now, more than ever, she knew that the two cases were connected.

Chapter 16

Vic got home from her rendezvous with Marion feeling out of sorts. She was physically satisfied but emotionally uncomfortable. She poured herself a glass of wine and told herself to get over it. She had what she wanted, casual sex, and that should be enough.

She sat down and checked her voicemail. "Speak of the devil," she said as she saw that Janey had left a message. It was only then that she realized how much she was thinking about her and why this afternoon with Marion fell short of making her happy.

Vic listened to the message.

"Hi, it's Janey. Sorry to bother you but I thought you'd want to know that Mom passed. I know you liked her and she loved you, more than me sometimes, I think. Just kidding. You know. Anyway there's going to be a service at Valhalla Chapel and the wake will be at my place. You're welcome to come. Actually, I would really like you to come. Oh, and the funeral is at 1:00 on Tuesday. You really were her favorite, you know.

Vic couldn't stop the tears running slowly down her cheek. Janey's mom, Lydia, truly was a wonderful woman. She was wrong though, Lydia loved Janey more than anyone in the whole world.

Vic would give anything to have the kind of relationship with her own mother that Janey had with Lydia. Lydia never even flinched when Janey came out to her. Vic's mom was devastated and angry when Vic told her she was a lesbian. Vic was so sure that her mom already had a clue, she never doubted her expectation of love and acceptance. She was wrong. Her mother had a look of disapproval--no, disgust, the likes of which Victoria, (her mom still won't call her Vic), had never seen.

Maybe if her father hadn't died the year before, things would have been different. Her father was too loving of a man to have disapproved of her for something as trivial as sexual preference. And it would not have mattered. "Follow your heart but don't forget your head," was one of his favorite sayings. And he had the ability to see what was in Vic's heart every day and twice on Sunday.

Her mother loved her, Vic didn't question that, but she always had ideas of who she wanted Vic to be. Vic sometimes worried that was not love at all.

There were the countless dresses that Vic was forced to wear. There was the frustration of her mother trying to get her to use makeup. Vic's friends begged their parents to let them wear makeup. Vic's mom pushed them on her like an Avon sales rep. It was a battle. It was always a battle.

When Vic was 8 she asked to join a softball team. Mom's answer was to enroll her in a modern dance class. Then there were was the hand-sewn dresses phase. Her mom fancied herself a seamstress but they were ugliest clothes that thoroughly embarrassed Vic to no end.

But with any battle there is an eventual winner. Sometimes Vic won. She played softball till she graduated from high school. Sometimes Vic lost. She wore silly, frilly dresses to Easter service every damn year.

When Vic finally decided to come out to her mother, she should have expected a battle, but Vic had been fighting with herself for so long, she thought the war was over. Sadly, it had just begun.

Her mother's first reaction was disgust, followed by anger, followed by hurt, followed by blame (anyone but herself), followed by D: all of the above.

Then came the denials. Denial that Vic was gay, denying Vic any opportunity to be close, in any way, to another girl. It seemed difficult for Vic to see how both denials could coexist but her mother made it happen. Every female friend she brought home was ushered out at the earliest opportunity.

There were no sleepovers EVER! Every boy at school became a potential boyfriend that Mom would all but shove in her face. And in high school, she insisted that Vic go on birth control pills. She would even give her condoms which Vic would then sell to her straight friends.

Things finally eased up after high school when her

older brother had a baby girl. Finally another female she could mold into the princess she had always wanted Vic to be.

When Vic was at college, she made the mistake of inviting a girlfriend to Christmas dinner. She was under the false impression that all the homophobia was now in the past, and she would be welcomed with open arms. In retrospect, she wondered why she was so blind to her mother's hatred. The incident was ugly and ended with a vow to never speak to each other again. It might have stayed that way if Vic hadn't dropped out of college. After getting her heart broken at school, Vic had to get away. She knew she should have just transferred but she was too broken to do the smart thing. Too broken still, she often thought. When she quit school she had no place to go, so she went home. Her mother agreed to take her in if she agreed to get "help" for her "affliction"... AKA conversion therapy. That was a nightmare.

For several weeks Vic was taught to hate who she was. They attempted to deconstruct her in an order to rebuild her as the perfect heterosexual being, the therapist believed everyone is born to be. In aversion therapy she would be shown lesbian themed images accompanied by shocks to the body. This was an attempt to forever associate homosexuality with pain. The tactic still haunts Vic, but she was lucky. When they started jamming Jesus down her throat, she knew it was time to leave.

It was actually a battle she won with her mother.

When she told her mother the details of the therapy, i.e. torture, her mother apologized and withdrew her demand that Vic endure this brutal treatment. Then the final solution was formed. "We just won't talk about it," was the agreement mother and daughter reached. And though far from perfect, it keeps them in each other's lives. It will never be as beautiful as what Janey had, but Vic could live with it.

Chapter 17

Vic woke up with a monster of a headache. She also woke up with spatters of blood on her tee shirt. Searching her body she found no cut to explain the blood. It took a minute before the memories of what happened surfaced to her conscious mind.

The blood was Marion's. The fog was lifting, replaced by shock. Slowly she pieced the night together.

She walked up to Marion's front door, but it was locked so she went around back to the back patio door which was conveniently unlocked. The house was dark except for a small light under the microwave in the kitchen. It was enough light for her to see her way to the staircase. She climbed the stairs toward the master bedroom. On the way she glanced at photos on the staircase wall and then down at her hand which held a .38 caliber pistol. She crept into the bedroom with confidence, walked up to the sleeping Marion and shot her twice in the head. It was cold, it was calculating, it was void of emotion.

None of this made any sense to Vic. She had no reason

to kill Marion. Her head was throbbing. Perhaps she was forgetting something, something that would have provoked her to commit such a horrific act. It wasn't like that time after college--that was self-defense. No, this was cold and calculating with no motivation whatsoever.

Vic started at the beginning, recollecting the night. She left for the bar rather late, but it was a Thursday night so it wouldn't be crowded. Vic found it best to let women have a few drinks before she approached them. Her interest in one night stands had dwindled since seeing Janey, and Marion filled certain primal needs. Still, Vic felt a different kind of need. A need for independence from commitment? Maybe a rejection of monogamy? It had something to do with the conversion therapy, but she had no interest in going to another kind of therapy to talk about her previous, so called, therapy. She knew it was unfair to compare psychotherapy with conversion therapy, but it was her excuse and she was sticking to it. Clearly, she still had trust issues.

The quest at the bar had not been a successful one. She spent more time talking to the gay guy on the next bar stool than she did talking up the ladies. That was all she could remember before Marion's house. She didn't recall having too much to drink, but it wouldn't be the first blackout she'd experienced.

Maybe it was a dream. Certainly the blood on her shirt was not a dream. However, there could be another explanation for it. Vic's headache was subsiding. Slowly she began to convince herself it was indeed a dream. The alternative was insane.

She decided, without much forethought, to call Marion. There was no answer so she decided to drive over to see her. The image of Marion lying in bed, bleeding from two bullet holes in her forehead and face, was ghastly. To think she was responsible for this horrific deed, made Vic sick to her stomach. She made her way down Marion's street trying not to vomit. She navigated the sharp curves and was struck by the view of several police cars in front of Marion's house, and cops in the front yard. Too late to turn around she cruised by as nonchalant as possible. Someone shouted, "There she is." Like a deer in the headlights, Vic's eyes got as big as saucers and she turned to see a man in the front yard pointing directly at her. Every single cop was looking her way.

She regained her fragile composure and hit the gas. In the rearview mirror Vic saw two cops getting into their vehicle, presumably to come after her.

The quick right, then a quick left, put her on the main thoroughfare. Checking her mirror again, there were no cop cars. Traffic was moderate and maneuverable. As Vic made another right, she caught a glimpse of a police car turning onto the thoroughfare she had just turned off of. Vic knew she had seconds to get away but she knew the city well, and driving a silver Prius allowed her to blend easily into traffic. Four blocks down, she got on the highway. Careful not to stay on the highway too long, she took the second exit.

Following the main drag took her from upper class neighborhoods to inner city poor. She felt like this would be an unlikely spot for the police to search for her until she realized her Prius stuck out like a sore thumb. She had to get some place where she could regroup. Maybe because Lydia had died recently, Vic thought of her abandoned house in south city. Vic still had a key to the house from the time she housesat with Janey. The attached garage would allow her to conceal her car. She could be there in ten minutes.

Vic arrived at Janey's mom's house without a hitch. A brief search found the garage door opener in a basket on the kitchen table. Much to her surprise, Lydia's car was still in the garage.

She thought at first she would swap it out with her own car until she realized an easier, perhaps safer way. You see, Lydia owned a silver Prius, almost identical to Vic's. Vic decided she could swap license plates instead. Since she had no keys for Lydia's car, she could now drive her own without the plates catching the eye of the police.

Chapter 18

Arthur walked into the bar, a stranger in a strange land. He hadn't anticipated the disparity in the number of women to men. It was a gay bar so, in his male privilege way, he assumed it would be mostly men. It never occurred to him that women would have their own bar.

He chose a bar stool near her, but not directly next to her. It took a while before he broke the ice with a mundane statement about the limited number of people at the establishment. The Campo woman nodded and muttered something about it getting busier as the night went on. Arthur searched for more conversation ideas as her disinterest was showing. Arthur was unaccustomed to a single woman, sitting at the bar, not being interested in any single men sitting near them.

Arthur decided on a political tack. "Can you believe what Trump tweeted today about banning transgenders from serving in the military?"

Bingo, Arthur got her attention.

"Leave it to the idiot-in-chief to sucker punch millions of Americans with his bigotry and hate." Campo was mildly incensed.

The problem with this approach was that Arthur knew little on the subject beyond the headlines. "Exactly! People serving our country and that's what they get."

Fortunately, that was enough to get Campo worked up into a mini tirade while Arthur cheered her on. Abruptly she left her seat, drink in hand. The time for Arthur to act was here, but her drink was not. Spontaneously he devised an alternative and ordered a vodka tonic. He quickly slipped a small packet of crushed Xanax into the cocktail.

When Campo returned, he slid the drink her way. "Hey, I think this is for you. I ordered another drink but the bartender gave me this by mistake. It's what you're drinking, right? Might as well not waste it. I mean, it's free. She already fixed my order." He held up his full glass to sell his story.

Vic was hesitant but it was a free drink from a gay brother so she snatched it up with a thank you.

It didn't take long to take effect. The Campo woman started being way more talkative and began to slur her words. For anyone watching, namely the bartender, she appeared to be intoxicated.

"You okay Vic?" The bartender leaned in and asked.

"Surrrre, I'm fine." She sighed "Well, maybe, kinda, not so much. Whaddya put in these things, beautiful?" Vic rested her chin in her right hand propped up by her elbow on the table.

The bartender smiled back and said "Maybe you should call it a night hun. You know the drill, give me your keys."

"OKay, no wait, I didn't drive. I Ubered it."

"I could give you a ride," Arthur inserted himself into the conversation.

Both women looked at him like he had just threatened their lives. Arthur immediately retracted that statement and suggested he call Uber for her. The women were much more receptive to that notion.

"Thass how I got here, thass how I'll leave." Vic was visibly and audibly inebriated.

By this time Campo's balance was less than stellar and Arthur offered to help her out to the nonexistent Uber car. Arthur had only pretended to order one on his phone. When they got outside Campo was very wobbly and getting her into Arthur's car was a challenge. She was willing, but her stupor made it difficult to shove her into the front seat.

Arthur knew exactly where she lived so his only concern was the drunk, or rather drugged, body seated next to him. She slumped against the door and Arthur shook her back to semi consciousness. They stumbled up to the front door. A neighbor stared disapprovingly. Arthur ignored him and tried to avoid facing him directly. He wouldn't want to have to kill him too. The neighbor retreated back into his apartment and Arthur finally got the door opened.

The rest was a breeze. He got her into bed where she

passed out immediately. He proceeded with the imprint and left through the front door before dawn.

Arthur arrived home early in the morning to "discover" his wife's lifeless body. He checked her pulse but did not touch anything but her wrist. He took a deep breath, worked himself into a good panic, and called the police.

"My wife's been shot! She isn't moving! I need an ambulance fast. What do I do? What do I do? I think she's dead!"

"Is there anyone in the house?"

"I don't know. I don't think so. Should I look?"

"No," the 911 operator said. "Sir, I want you to go outside and wait for the police. Stay on the phone with me. We are sending a squad car now."

Before Arthur did as he was told, He splashed water on his face and rubbed his eyes vigorously to give the impression that he'd been crying. He wiped the sinister grin off his face, as well.

When the police arrived most of them went in the house but two plain clothed cops approached Arthur and introduced themselves. No introduction was actually necessary; Arthur recognized them as the ones who came to his house after Carver's death.

"We need to ask you a few questions." The male detective, Schwartz, started asking standard questions, to all of which Arthur had standard answers.

It soon became apparent that Schwartz had a more sympathetic view. Bailey, on the other hand, looked like she was ready to haul his ass away to jail toot sweet. Eventually, Schwartz asked the question Arthur had been waiting for.

"Mr. Murdoch, can you think of anyone who wanted to hurt your wife?"

"That woman! I can't think of anyone else." Arthur feigned anger.

"What woman?" Bailey interjected. Bailey lifted her pen off her note pad, furrowed her brow and glared at Murdoch. Every fiber in her body told her this man was not as he seemed.

"A woman friend. No," he paused and bit down on his lower lip. "Not a friend, a lover."

Bailey intensified her line of questioning. "That must have made you very angry. Understandably, really. Nothing stings quite like betrayal." Not leaving any room for his reply, she continued. "You confronted her with this? How did that go? Not good, I imagine."

Arthur was taken aback by how quickly Bailey pivoted and started aiming her arrows at him. He should have predicted that but thankfully Schwartz took the bait.

Much to the Bailey's dismay Schwartz turned the conversation back towards "that woman." "Why do you think this woman would want to hurt your wife?" Sensing his partner's displeasure he added, "This woman have a name?"

This was not why Bailey was upset, but Schwartz was clueless.

"My wife had become afraid of her. She wouldn't say

exactly why but she had knowledge of something that woman had done. I got the impression it was something illegal."

"You let it go at that?" Bailey asked skeptically. She took a mental step back as she knew this grilling should be taking place in an interrogation room, not literally, in his own front yard. At the station, Bailey had the power. With that she decided to let him finish his explanation and perhaps he would hang himself with it.

Without answering the detectives' question, Arthur got back to his monologue. "I told her we should call the police, but she said she was just being paranoid. I was upset about the affair so the conversation turned to us."

"And what did you decide?" Schwartz inquired.

"We decided to work harder on our marriage. She said I've been working too much and she felt neglected. She had a point. Bottom line, we were getting past it and, frankly, I think we are, uh, were closer than we had been years."

"Was she still seeing the mystery woman?" Bailey rejoined the conversation. "Do you know her name?"

Arthur had thought long and hard about whether to divulge the full name. In doing so, he would probably have to disclose hiring a private investigator. "Marion called her Vic. That's all I know."

The crime scene unit was done with their inspection of the house. They were all out on the lawn and driveway along with Bailey, Schwartz and Murdoch.

Suddenly Arthur spotted Vic cruising slowly past the

house. "There she is!" he screamed, pointing his finger at the silver car. Arthur could never have expected such a welcome surprise, he could not have scripted it better.

Bailey instructed a uniform cop to follow the car but he was slow to get going. Fortunately, a different officer was able to get the license plate number.

The detectives seemed unconcerned that his wife's killer was getting away. This made Arthur nervous, perhaps for the first time. They asked Arthur a few more exasperating questions before finally leaving.

"A third murder! For fuck's sake, a third murder!" Bailey exclaimed as they pulled away from the Murdoch home.

"C'mon Gwen. We don't know whether all three are connected," Schwartz responded. "They got the guy in the Jankowski case."

"Really, Danny? Do I have to draw you a map?" Gwen didn't like to lash out at her partner but this case just got weirder.

Schwartz knew it was time to change the subject, to focus on the case at hand. "The guys found the gun in the house. CSU got prints on it too, .38 caliber."

"Hmm, same as the Carver case," Bailey noted.

"It's already on its way to ballistics. I'll put a rush on it," Danny said emphatically.

Schwartz got a call and relayed the information to Bailey, "The car is registered to Victoria Campo on South Grand."

"Sounds like our next destination."

Chapter 19

Vic's head was swimming with memories and fears. There was so much she couldn't comprehend. Questioning your own memories is a logically impossible task. If your memory is forcing you to ask a question, your answer would be based on the same memory. Swimming indeed.

"Sort it out. Break it down," Vic spoke to herself. The most puzzling of things was the why of it all. There was nothing in her relationship with Marion that would warrant such violence. It seemed obvious to Vic that something took place between the bar and Marion's house. It couldn't have been in person or else she wouldn't have found her asleep in her own bed. Vic checked her phone but there were no calls or texts since yesterday afternoon. The memory of Marion's murder played in a never-ending loop of horror.

Something, suddenly, caught Vic's attention. How did she know the layout of the house, in particular the location of the master bedroom? She distinctly remembered going straight to the stairwell from the patio entrance as if she had been there many times. Heading up the stairs she noticed the family photos on the wall and the odd placement of a mirror. Then it struck Vic! The reflection in the mirror was not hers. For that matter the hand holding the gun seem much larger than her hand. As she focused her mind on the mirror, she knew what she was seeing. It was the man in Marion's front yard pointing his finger at Vic. This made no sense to her. Perhaps the mirror was really just a picture on the wall of the man who Vic presumed to be the husband. However that didn't explain the hand that did not seem at all a part of her body. It was larger, older, a man's hand. She tried to focus on more detail but the reflection was fuzzy. Her heart lept at the possibility that crept into her mind. Perhaps she was not the killer. Perhaps she was a witness. But how would a witness see from someone else's viewpoint?

The headache from this morning had returned with a vengeance. It made it incredibly difficult to focus on anything. There was no food in the house, so Vic decided to risk going to the market. Hopefully, the license plate swap solution would pass its first test.

She returned from the store unscathed. After making herself something to eat, she started over. When she got to the reflection in the mirror, she was certain that it was not a photo and that it was the man in Marion's front yard. Vic needed to verify who it was and turned to Google. Several images of Arthur Murdock appeared confirming his identity and Vic's presumption that it was, indeed, Marion's husband. One photo seemed more familiar than the other. As she searched her memory it came to her. Put a goatee and glasses on that photo and you have the guy from the bar. Vic was sure of it.

For the first time that day Vic questioned her guilt. She was no closer to an explanation, but clearly things were not as cut-and-dry as her initial memories seemed to be. With her new found hope, Vic decided to try and get sleep. Sleep did not come and she decided on a new direction. She would go back to the bar from the night before and see if anything came back to her, and more importantly, see if someone else had a better memory than her.

She got to the bar and the place was jammed on a Friday night. She checked behind the bar but her tattooed bartender was nowhere in sight. When she asked to her whereabouts she was told it was her night off. Per the older freckled bartender, Maddy, the tattooed bartender, would be back tomorrow night.

Victoria decided she would come back the next day when Maddy started her shift. She meandered through the crowd, questioning people she knew. Only one person had seen her the night before and all she could recall was seeing her sitting at the bar chatting with some guy. Vic pressed for more details but none was forthcoming. In the end it was a fruitless trip and left Vic frustrated.

Chapter 20

Bailey and Schwartz arrived at Victoria Campo's apartment around noon. Campo was not home but the landlord let them in. Nothing stood out. There was a fair amount of clutter in the living room. The bed had been slept in but nothing to determine when. The kitchen was neat and tidy except for the overflowing recycling bin. In short, it was ordinary. No gun. No suspect. No secret panel with stalker photos you might see, according to Hollywood, in a serial killer's home.

The mail on the coffee table offered little insight. Apparently she was late on her electric bill and there was a dart tournament coming up at a bar called "Attitudes." Campo was only a person of interest, there was no arrest warrant so their search was limited to items in plain sight.

Bailey sent Schwartz to canvass the neighbors. He came back with a middle-aged black man with a beer gut, in tow. "Thought you might want to have a word with Mr. Davis. He says he saw Campo come home last night."

"Mr. Davis, hello. I'm detective Bailey. So you saw Miss Campo last night?"

"Sure did," Davis replied.

"What time was that?"

"Not sure, before midnight though. I'm sure of that," Davis said confidently.

"How is that?" Bailey continued.

"I was watching Colbert. Then I went to bed. Well, I grabbed my mail just before, that's when I saw them."

"Them? Miss Campo was not alone?"

"No. There was a guy with her."

"A guy?" Schwartz interrupted, letting his surprise show.

"I know, right. Never seen her come home with a guy before. Then again she was drunk, so anything goes, right?"

"Did you recognize the man?"

"No, just some guy. I've never seen him before."

"What makes you think she was drunk?" Bailey asked.

"I don't know, maybe cuz I'm not stupid." Davis clearly took offense.

"I'm sorry sir, go ahead," Bailey tried to change her tone to accommodate the witness.

"Well she was stumbling all over and her speech was all messed up. She turned to say hi and nearly fell over, 'cept the guy was holding her up."

"What did the guy look like?"

"Kind of ordinary, white, not very tall, dark hair, glasses, beard. Well, more like a goatee."

Bailey and Schwartz glanced at each to see if the description was at all familiar. It was not.

Looking back to the witness Bailey continued, "What was he doing?"

"Helping her get inside. I did worry some. Like I said, she never brings home guys, if you know what I mean." Mr. Davis lowered his tone as if he was about to divulge a great secret. "She's a lesbian." He paused for dramatic effect before saying, "Not that I care. No judgement here. None of my business."

Bailey sensed that none of those last statements were true. He cared, he judged and he made it his business.

"Did it look like they were together, a couple?" Schwartz interjected.

"Couldn't say. Don't think so but really couldn't say." Davis was being aloof now, perhaps in response to the disapproving look Bailey had shot him.

They concluded their interview and began discussing it with each other in the car.

Schwartz began, "seems odd, don't you think? Came home drunk, goes out later to kill Mrs. Murdoch."

"Odd, indeed. And who is our mystery man? Didn't sound like anyone we know, did it?" Bailey asked rhetorically.

"Maybe the coroner's estimated time of death is wrong. Maybe Campo and mystery man already killed Murdoch," Schwartz postulated.

"If Bailey was as drunk as the neighbor said, that possibility seems unlikely." Bailey added her own speculation, "Then again, maybe she killed Murdoch and drank her remorse. Danny, check with the coroner and see if he can narrow down the time of death. Ballistics should have something for us tomorrow."

"Aren't we due in court this afternoon in the Johnson case?" Schwartz said anxiously.

"Shit, I forgot," Bailey exclaimed. "Heading there now."

Chapter 21

Vic arrived at the bar just after three when the bartender, Maddy, started her shift. She had spent the night searching her mind for more details, to no avail. It was like a broken record playing the same memories over and over again, no more, no less. She felt as if there was footage missing from the movie in her mind, forever lost.

Maddy was busy behind the bar but looked up to greet Vic. "Hey you, you're here awfully early. What can I get you?"

"Some peace of mind I hope," she said with a painful half smile on her face.

"Don't know that drink," she said sarcastically. "Gonna have to check my handy dandy bartender's guide for that one."

Vic chuckled half-heartedly, "Haha. No, I was here the night before last and I've got a bit of a problem with my memory."

"Did something happen? Was it that guy?" Maddy was deathly serious now.

"You remember that guy?" Vic was excited.

"You know, at first, I thought he wasn't right, but it got busy," the bartender said with a tinge of guilt.

"What do you remember? Anything could help," Vic pleaded.

"Well, you were sitting at your regular bar stool, keeping to yourself. Then this guy came in and sat down at the end of the bar. At first, I thought he was in the wrong place, but he was too relaxed to be a straight guy who accidentally walked into a gay bar. Next thing, you two were chatting it up. Then the booze must have hit you, cuz next thing, you were hammered."

"Damn, how long had I been there?"

"Not that long. I was kinda surprised. Then the guy offered to give you a ride, but I nixed that." Maddy seemed pleased with herself momentarily. "Instead he called Uber."

"Sooooo, the driver came and I left? Did I leave alone?" Vic urged.

"That's the thing. I got busy and you were gone when I next checked. Vic, I'm really sorry. He seemed harmless, but I should have been more careful," Maddy said apologetically.

Vic tried to reassure her, "It's not your fault."

Unnecessarily contrite, Maddy added, "I stopped serving you as soon as I noticed you were drunk, but it happened so fast."

Vic was perplexed, "Kinda surprising. I don't usually get so drunk so fast."

"True, nobody can call you a lightweight." Maddy regretted that observation immediately.

"I can't argue that. What if, oh my god, what if the jerk slipped me a roofie? Maybe he drugged me." While most people would have been incredibly disturbed by the possibility, Vic was encouraged that this could explain a lot.

The bartender was more upset about it than Vic was. "He called Uber, or rather used an app. Asked for the bar address and everything. You could call and find out if they sent a driver and where he took you."

"Great idea. Don't beat yourself up Maddy. I'll get to the bottom of this. It's okay, look I'm still alive and kicking." Vic sensed her remorse and sought to reassure her but her smile was forced. "Thanks for everything."

Vic headed for the door, brushing against the rather attractive woman on the way. As Vic opened the door she heard the woman's voice behind her, "Victoria Campo?" It was the cops. It had to be, Vic thought. Run was the only other thought in her head so she took off, running out the door and to her car.

Detective Bailey and Schwartz rushed toward the door only to run into a brick wall named JD. JD was a bouncer and she was built for the part. Not tall, but wide bodied with broad shoulders and thick arms. The detectives tried to sidestep the bouncer but she was immovable. The cops identified themselves but JD demanded to see their badges.

"How about I show you my handcuffs instead?" Bailey said emphatically. Reluctantly, the bouncer dropped her arms and stepped aside. Bailey and Schwartz darted outside, but their suspect was gone.

The adrenaline was coursing through her veins as she headed toward her hideout, such as it was. She had barely escaped twice now, and she knew her luck would eventually run out. For now, however, she made it home safely. So busy with getting there, she didn't notice the car in front of Lydia's house, aka Vic's safe haven. She did however, notice Janey startled and staring at her in the kitchen when Vic entered via the back door. Her heart seemed to clench like a fist. In fear, in joy, in both.

"What the fuck are you doing here?" Janey blurted out.

There was no way for Vic to adequately answer that question in less than a thousand words. She went with the most succinct, "Hiding from the police," she said quietly as her words trailed off. Vic wasn't sure what to expect, rage or concern.

She got neither at first with Janey responding with an equally succinct "I see." They both stood in silence until Janey finally spoke, "An explanation would be nice."

Vic tried to start at the beginning, but the beginning kept changing. Strangely enough, it was harder for Vic to explain her affair with Marion than talking about how she may have murdered her. But perhaps the strangest thing for Vic was Janey's matter-of-fact response.

"You didn't kill anyone," Janey said flatly.

Somehow, Janey saying it made it all the more possible for Vic to believe it. Everything seemed possible again.

The despair that had been toying with her mind lifted like the sun peering out from the clouds on a dismal day. After pouring out every last detail, they talked about the facts like they were solving a mystery in a Hollywood movie. Could it be this, could it be that?

The most intriguing idea came from Janey. "I was thinking about when I quit smoking. I used hypnosis. Perhaps the dick at the bar hypnotized you. Assuming he drugged you, you might be more receptive to hypnosis."

"So I killed her while in a hypnotic trance?" To Vic that was no more comforting than the original idea of the crime of passion. Certainly no less culpable in the eyes of the law.

"Maybe, but I was thinking more like...he hypnotized you into believing you killed Mary Ann."

"Marion."

"Whatever."

Was that jealousy Vic detected in Janey's voice? Vic smiled.

"So what's our plan?" Janey said deviously.

"OUR plan! No, Janey, this is my problem, NOT yours! WE don't do anything. The most you can do is leave and not tell the cops where I am!" Vic said adamantly.

"Okay, now that you have your self-sacrificing speech out of the way, shall we get down to figuring this shit out." Janey said as she stared intently at Vic.

Vic started to renew her objections but something stopped her. Janey made it seem like the reasonable and logical thing to do. Yes, "work together to figure this shit out" as Janey so aptly put it.

So Vic dug in, "Well, first I need to contact Uber to find out if somebody picked me up and where they took me."

"Do you know how to do that?" Janey inquired.

"Not a clue. Literally clueless."

"I was thinking." Janey narrowed her eyes and gazed mischievously at Vic. "Do you think that bartender is going to tell the cops the same thing she told you about the guy and Uber?"

Vic didn't know where Janey was going but she was eager to hear. "I'm guessing she would. She felt pretty bad about the whole situation."

"Hello, this is Detective...Boysenberry." Janey said with horrendous British accent.

Vic let out a good belly laugh. "Boysenberry? Really?"

"Okay, perhaps Detective Briscoe. Lenny always was my favorite on Law & Order," Janey said, still smiling.

"Alright Det. Briscoe, what are you up to?" Vic was loving this.

"So... I bet if I called Uber and said I was detective Boysen, uh, Briscoe, they might be inclined to tell me what we need to know."

Vic was impressed. "I think Detective Boysenberry is on to something." Vic started to question why Janey should make the call but thought better of it. Instead she changed topics. "I like your idea of hypnosis. I think I should look into the science of it and see what I can find out."

"Excellent idea," Janey added, "seems like what they show in the movies is a little far-fetched but maybe this Murdoch jerk is especially good at it."

Vic thought more and more about the hypnosis angle and although the idea seemed unlikely, it still made for a reasonable answer to this number one question in all of this. Why would she kill Marion? On the other hand, if Arthur Murdoch knew about the affair he might possess enough rage to kill his wife. Vic was biased, but he seemed a much more likely murderer than her.

Vic and Janey spent the evening talking and occasionally laughing, momentarily forgetting the dire situation at hand. Eventually things got awkward and Janey said, reluctantly for sure, "I should go."

Vic drew her close and kissed her gently on the lips. "Stay, please stay."

Janey stayed.

Chapter 22

Bailey's instincts told her one thing but the evidence told her something entirely different. The prints came back and they belonged to Victoria Campo. Her's were the only prints on the gun. Ballistics showed that this same gun was used in both the Marion Murdoch murder and Martin Carver's murder. Campo was on the run which implies guilt but Bailey knew that innocent women can run just as hard as guilty ones. Nonetheless, Bailey's gut told her the investigation should be focused on Arthur Murdoch.

She and Schwartz had gone to the bar on the flyer they found at Campo's apartment. It had proved fruitful but not to substantiate the current working theory. Instead it turned up contrary evidence, namely, the mystery man at the bar and then again at Campo's apartment. The Uber office confirmed that no driver was sent to the bar and the neighbor's account made it seem like the mystery man took her home by himself. Even if Bailey went with the logical interpretation that they hooked up, that didn't sit well. A lesbian at a lesbian bar does not pick up a man. There are exceptions, but the bartender's story doesn't indicate a hookup at all.

Bailey followed that thought with the notion that Campo did not go willingly with the man, or perhaps she was too drunk to consent. This, however, would make her the victim, not the perp.

But what if Campo sobered up and reached out to her girlfriend, Marion, for comfort or companionship and instead got rejection. Maybe Arthur Murdoch was telling the truth about his wife and their desire to repair their marriage. Not likely, Bailey thought.

Yet, none of that felt right. Arthur Murdoch was a total sleaze bag and the logical suspect. Maybe the mystery man was supposed to...supposed to what? Bailey aborted that train of thought. No, let the evidence be your guide was Bailey's motto. She needed to find Victoria Campo, now.

And Bailey wasn't the only one. Arthur needed Victoria Campo found, too. The detectives had been back once already and seemed more interested in him than his wife's killer, or rather, Arthur's patsy. There was no murder/imprint solution to this problem. Murder Bailey? Murder Schwartz? Murder Campo?

Arthur knew it was dangerous to think he could simply kill people that got in his way, but it didn't stop the thoughts from popping into his head.

Arthur decided to take matters into his own hands. There was some risk involved but the current situation was untenable. He called his private investigator and rehired her to find Campo, now.

Chapter 23

Janey showed up at her mom's house with news and take out in hand. Vic was well past antsy and on to bouncing off the walls when Janey arrived. The anxiety lessened immediately, replaced by comfort in the midst of chaos. They greeted each other with hugs and slightly hesitant kisses.

They sat at the kitchen table as if it were a working lunch with plastic containers of their favorite pasta littered about. Vic felt like she could eat it all herself, although she hadn't been hungry all day. But having Janey there made everything seem normal.

"So Det. Boysenberry was successful," Janey proclaimed.

Vic was not so eager to leave the moment of blissful ignorance she was enjoying. If she didn't think about it, it wouldn't be real.

Too late. Janey mentioned the fictional Det. Boysenberry and it all came roaring back. She was in a corner, in a cage, there was no way out. The notion of turning herself in became more and more appealing every day. Just make it end, Victoria thought while fighting back tears. The limbo she was hiding in was taking its toll. If she surrendered, the constant fear of discovery would be gone. However, the alternative of being pushed thru the criminal justice system, ending in years in prison was unpalatable. Vic's misery was showing.

"Earth to Vic. Honey, we'll get through this. I promise," Janey said gently.

"Don't make promises you can't keep." Vic spoke sharply.

Instantly regretting her words, she apologized. "I'm sorry. I'm just not feeling it right now. So what did you find out?"

"That's the spirit," Janey said cheerfully. "All right. I called Uber and it was actually much easier than I thought. No request was received and no driver was dispatched. So that means...hmm, what does that mean?"

Vic had the answer for that question. "It means I'm not losing my mind. You know I would never hookup with a man, sober or drunk. So that means I was coerced at best, kidnapped at worst. He definitely drugged me. That had to be his plan."

"The plan to hypnotize you? Get you drunk, sorry, spike your drink, get you into his car and hypnotize you? Is that what we're saying here?"

Vic didn't care for Janey's skepticism. "Maybe there are some gaps in the time line but now that I know I was not in control of my own actions, I can make certain assumptions. Primarily, women who have been slipped a roofie do not have the wherewithal to plan and commit a murder." There was positivity in her voice.

Janey jumped in. "So if the hypnosis concept is correct, he hypnotized you into believing you killed Marion, NOT actually killing her."

Janey sounded relieved, and Vic knew it but decided to let it slide. It would be unfair for her to presume Janey was entirely without doubts.

"That makes sense." Vic was excited to make another connection, "I looked into hypnosis and the general consensus amongst scientists is that a person can not be hypnotized into committing a crime. That said, there are some hypnotists who say it is possible but they are very rare cases where the defendant claimed they committed crimes under hypnosis, but it rarely worked, and they were many years ago."

"That seems a little ambiguous," Janey sounded disappointed.

"Actually the scientists, who say it's not possible, give the reason you can only be hypnotized into doing something you were already inclined to do. Like a serial killer might be hypnotized to kill again. Soooo, since I was not inclined to kill Marion and I'm not a serial killer... it means I didn't kill her. Does that make sense?"

"Kinda," Janey lacked confidence in her words. "Of course, that is all predicated on you being hypnotized, and that's just a guess." Jenny asked the next unwanted question. "What if you weren't hypnotized at all?"

"Maybe I hypnotized myself." Vic got a deservedly strange look for her statement. "Maybe it was more like traumatized, instead of hypnotized. I witnessed the crime, so I guilted myself into believing I committed the crime."

Janey didn't like being the contrary voice on that one. "Why would he drug you, kidnap you, take you to his house? So you can watch him kill his wife?"

"What if that's how he does it?" Vic postulated. "Traumatizes his victims, then hypnotizes them."

"But that is the exact opposite of what hypnotists do. They try to calm you down, relax you, put you in a suggestive state." Janey added, "That's what they did with me and my cigarette cessation hypnosis."

Janey and Vic went back and forth, bouncing ideas off of each other, but never really got beyond the theory of her being hypnotized into believing she had killed Marion. Besides that's what they both wanted to believe.

"So, say this is true," Janey stared curiously at Vic. "What do we do?"

"We have to tell the police." Vic hesitated, saddened by the next obvious fact. "But they would never believe me."

Janey agreed, "You need proof."

"Easier said than done." Vic said, resigning herself to the foregone conclusion that the cops wouldn't buy hypnosis for a second. Vic needed real proof. "I've got to confront him, get him to confess." Vic stated concisely.

"He went to all that trouble to set you up, yet you think he will confess to the police?"

"Not the police. Just me." Vic continued, "I get him to talk. I record it. I pass it on to the police." Vic slapped her hand down on the table as if it was a done deal.

"Are you nuts?" Janey shrieked.

"I'll be safe. Maybe do it at his work. Hmm, I wonder where he works?" Vic grabbed her tablet, eager to get to work on her plan for Arthur Murdoch.

Janey was rambling on about the insanity of her idea while Vic was looking up Arthur online. She was not prepared for the barrage of headlines about Marion's murder. One headline stood out.

Marion Murdoch:
Murder Suspect Turned Murder Victim

Vic had no idea that Marion was about to stand trial for the murder of her father. Marion had never said a word. She read the article to Janey whose face glazed over with astonishment.

"I never would have pegged Marion for a murderer," Vic stated. "Plus, she adored her father."

"Funny how she confessed to something you don't think she was capable of doing. Hmm, sound like anyone we know?" Janey pointed her finger directly at Vic.

"Good god!!! You don't think he hypnotized Marion too!" By the time Vic finished that sentence, it was exactly what they both thought.

"All the more reason you steer clear of this psychopath." Janey demanded.

"All the more reason I confront him. I bring up Marion and hypnosis, he thinks I'm onto him, bingo, he spills the beans!"

"Or thinks you're on to him and spills your blood!"

"You got a better idea?" Vic asked, and Janey said nothing.

In Vic's mind it was settled. In Janey's mind it was still up for debate. And so they debated until Janey acquiesced.

They decided on a stealthy approach. Meeting him in public would just be inviting him to scream for the police. It would be best if she approached him alone and by surprise.

Chapter 24

Vic left the safety of the hideout prepared to do battle. She was inundated with a level of nervousness that only presents itself in extreme situations. Confronting a killer, armed with only a tape recorder and golf club, definitely qualified as an extreme situation.

Her stomach was in a knot. As she rehearsed her lines she stumbled over her words. Vic reminded herself why she was here. The only way to escape the web that Arthur Murdoch had spun was to face him head on, steadfast in her resolve. She must not let him win this battle.

Vic approached the back door. It was unlocked. She headed for the staircase. The eerie familiarity was not lost on Vic. She knew this house, though firmly believed she had never been there. There was a light in the master bedroom. She approached with a golf club in hand.

Arthur was startled at first but then let out a loud guffaw. "You've come to kill me with a golf club. At least it's original."

Vic was mildly embarrassed. She didn't own a gun

and she wanted something she could wield from a distance. She was counting on him not wanting her dead, he needs her to take the fall for Marion's murder. It just dawned on Vic, Arthur could blow her away and claim self-defense against an intruder. Fortunately, Arthur did not have a gun and was in no position, sitting up in bed, to fight against an angry woman with a golf club.

"I'm not here to kill you. I'm here to let you know the jig is up, asshole. I know what you did to me! And I know you did the same thing to Marion." Vic still had her doubts but doubts had no place here.

"Pray tell, what do you think I did?" Arthur said smugly.

"You hypnotized us into believing we killed somebody when it was really you," Vic said emphatically.

Arthur didn't flinch. "What a strange imagination you have. Livin' in a fantasy world, are you?"

"You drugged me at the bar, that's no fantasy. I have proof of that."

This time Arthur flinched, "Not likely. Unless you ran and got a blood test, you couldn't possibly have proof."

Vic was hopeful. It wasn't a confession, but it was close. "Maybe I did. I knew right away I'd been drugged."

"Maybe? You just admitted you didn't." Arthur chuckled. "Besides, you can't prove you didn't take the Xanax yourself."

"Funny, I didn't mention Xanax." It was Vic's turn to be smug.

"Even if you could prove I drugged you, the cops

would never believe I hypnotized you." Arthur went from smug to cocky. "I'll give you credit though, you're close, but you have no idea what I'm capable of." Arthur desperately wanted to brag about his gift.

"Now it's my turn. Pray tell, explain it to me." Vic said mockingly.

"I think not. I think I'll let you try to convince the cops I hypnotized you," Arthur said.

"And Marion, don't forget what you did to her!" Vic was losing sight of her goal, getting angry instead.

"Which part, imprinting on her or blowing her brains out?" He laughed sardonically. "I think it's time for you to tell your ridiculous story to the police."

Arthur slowly reached for his phone keeping one eye on Vic.

Vic moved in swiftly and wham! Vic's golf club came crashing down on Arthur's phone, smacking it into little pieces. Arthur drew his knees up an assumed a defensive position with his arms covering his head. Vic had given herself the time she needed and made a beeline for the back door. By the time she got in her car Arthur was just a few yards behind her.

He stood defiant. "This doesn't change anything. The police still aren't going to believe your fairy tale."

"But they'll believe this! I got you on tape, mother fucker! You are toast!"

Arthur turned ghostly white. He was frozen in panic.

Meanwhile, Vic drove away leaving him blank-faced on his front lawn.

Chapter 25

Bailey and Schwartz finally got a hold of Mrs. Campo, who had been out of town. She was genuinely surprised to see the police at her door, even more so to learn they were looking for her daughter. Mrs. Campo had not seen, nor heard from, her daughter in several weeks and gave no reason for the detectives to think she was lying. She was forthcoming with some basic information the detectives already possessed, but when asked about friends or girlfriends, only one name came up. Janey Newcombe. Per Mrs. Campo, Janey was Victoria's girlfriend a while back but she wasn't certain they were still in touch. She didn't have an address but she knew the neighborhood, Dogtown, so the police database provided the rest.

When they arrived at Jane Newcombe's home, she was just getting home from work.

After routine introductions, Bailey spoke, "Ms. Newcombe, I understand you know Victoria Campo?"

"I do, well, mostly I did." Janey continued, "We are no longer together."

Their conversation was short but Bailey had reservations about the truthfulness in Newcombe's answers. For one thing Newcombe never asked why the police were looking for her supposedly ex-girlfriend. In addition, Bailey felt she was being evasive about when she saw Campo last. The detectives left, making a phone call before driving away.

Janey was a bundle of nerves after the cops left. She wanted to run to Vic and tell her all about it. She was confident she hadn't given anything away to the police but she was uneasy just the same. She grabbed a few things and headed for the "hideout" as Vic called it. Still nervous about the police, Janey drove cautiously, diligently keeping an eye out for cops. It didn't take long for Janey to notice a black sedan that appeared to be following her. She put it to the test with a few superfluous turns.

The black sedan matched her movements turn for turn, confirming her suspicions. Janey spotted a grocery store and decided to pull over. The black sedan passed her and turned at the stop sign. At first Janey thought perhaps she was just being paranoid, however, after buying a few items at the store she came out to find the black sedan parked a few cars down on the opposite side of the street.

Janey decided not to take any chances so she returned home. She couldn't call Vic. Vic had long since ditched her phone in a trash can. GPS is not your friend when you are wanted by the police.

So Janey sat in front of her TV worrying terribly about her girlfriend. Janey smiled at the idea of thinking of Vic that way again. Their last time around had been so strong, or so Janey thought, then in an instant Vic was gone. Her head told her to avoid the chance of repeating history at all costs, but her heart had convinced her head that this time was different.

Janey knew Vic was going to break in to the Murdoch house to execute her "record a confession" plan. Janey had planned on talking her out of it but it was just too risky to go to her, for now. So Janey waited till 3 a.m. before sneaking out. She peaked through the living room curtains, looking for the familiar black sedan. Unfortunately, in the middle of the night, on a dimly lit city street, every other car looks like a black sedan. Her car was parked right out front so there was no way to slip past any surveillance. So she slipped out the back, walked down to the corner bar and called a cab, using a phony name. When she got to the hideout Vic wasn't there. Janey rightfully assumed Vic was still at her rendezvous with Arthur Murdoch.

Vic's heart was pounding with the thrill of victory diminished only by the residual fear from her encounter with Arthur Murdoch. If only Janey were here with her, she could calm her down. Well, only after she regaled her with her victorious adventure at the home of a killer. Vic would have to relish her success alone.

It was the second time Janey surprised Vic in the

kitchen of the hideout. This time there was no hesitation, Vic ran to her and threw her arms around her and squeezed. She planted a big kiss on her lips and shouted "I did it! I got it! We can get this to the police and it's over." Vic pulled the recorder out of her pocket clenched in her fist.

Janey was ecstatic. "He admitted hypnotizing you or killing Marion?"

"Both! It was unfuckingbelievable," Vic said excitedly. "He was so cocky, he told me as if he was just waiting for me to ask." Vic sat down and started fiddling with the recorder. "Here, I'll play it for you." Vic hit the play button.

"*Testing 123, testing.*" Vic smiled at the sound of her own voice. She listened at the sounds of scuffling in her pocket till Arthur's voice began "*You've come to kill me with a golf club. At least it's original. I'm not here to kill you. I'm here to let you know the jig is up...*" A series of clicks followed and then silence.

Absolute silence.

Vic screamed, "No, this can't be happening!" Vic slid the power button off then on again. The same thirty seconds played over again and then stopped, just as before. She hit rewind. She hit fast forward. The recorder had two separate recording channels, A and B. She had recorded on A so she went to B and tested again.

Everything worked fine but no matter what she did, the recorded confession did not exist. Vic was distraught. In an instant, the light at the end of the tunnel had been extinguished. She sobbed in despair as Janey hugged her and sobbed with her.

Risk is only as wise as the payoff, and right now Vic couldn't feel more foolish.

Chapter 26

Maddy, the bartender, came into the station begging for a chance to work with a sketch artist. Bailey thought it might be helpful so she obliged. Hours later, the police artist dropped off his rendition of the mystery man. Sadly, Bailey didn't recognize him but there was something familiar about him. Facial recognition was not Bailey's strong suit, that was Schwartz' area of expertise. Schwartz did not disappoint. One glance at the sketch and Danny recognized Arthur Murdoch. Once he removed the beard and added glasses, Bailey could see it too.

Bailey had theorized before that Campo might be a victim but this solidified that assumption. In fact, this was really the first evidence they had that linked Arthur Murdoch to his wife's murder.

Bailey needed confirmation that only the bartender and neighbor could provide. She needed them to identify Murdoch as the mystery man and for that she needed to setup a lineup. She didn't have enough evidence to arrest

Murdoch so she was going to have to convince him to do it voluntarily.

Bailey and Schwartz arrived unannounced at Carver Industries after lunch. Murdoch was hoping they were there to inform him of Campo's capture, yet he quickly realized that was not their intent.

"We just have a couple of questions," Bailey began.

"Well, I only have one. Why haven't you caught that Campo woman yet?" Arthur insinuated incompetence.

Bailey ignored his question and continued with her own. "You said you were working late the night of your wife's death, correct?"

Arthur nodded. "Yes I was, and I've told you that many times."

"It's just that we have witnesses that someone fitting your description was seen in the company of Victoria Campo that night." Bailey stated firmly.

"That's just not possible!" Arthur said emphatically. "I've never met her. I repeat. I was at work! Then I went to the diner. I have the receipt. Actually, I've shown you the receipt."

Bailey clearly got a rise out of Murdoch, but it was not accompanied by any wavering in his story. "That's true, you were clearly at the diner. Mr. Murdoch, we can resolve this misunderstanding easily enough. If you came in for a lineup, we could clear this up and be done with it."

Arthur was reticent but his overconfidence took him right down the path Bailey led him to and he agreed to come in for a lineup.

Bailey made a few calls and set it up for that evening. Both the bartender and the neighbor agreed to participate. The downside is that they weren't allowed to add the beard for identification purposes. They were, however, allowed to add the glasses but that didn't help. Maddy, the bartender, picked out the wrong guy, and the neighbor just couldn't be sure.

Det. Bailey begrudgingly let Murdoch go. This case was definitely getting under her skin.

On the other side, Arthur was proud of himself for not letting his confidence waiver despite the obvious attempt by the police. Admittedly, he was confused, or perhaps just concerned, with what information the police had. The witnesses had to be bar patrons, most likely the bartender. And then there's the neighbor. Clearly they did not have the recording, or he'd be in jail. The only reason he could fathom for Campo not turning over the recording was fear. The police are notoriously single-minded, and she may feel like once in their grasp, they may not let go.

Any way he looked at it, he had to see the recording never got into the hands of the police. And the only way to do that was to get his hands on it first. That part was clear but first Arthur had to admit something had gone awry with the imprint. Even if Campo didn't know the details, she knew the memories were not her own. The second imprint on Marion was the only other attempt that had failed but she was never aware that the attempt was even made.

Campo called it hypnosis and Arthur could see why but he had difficulty understanding how she knew it was anything at all. He reviewed in his mind and found the only possible explanation. The imprint is initiated during sleep, but Campo was more like passed out. A drug induced sleep might lessen the effects. Arthur saw this as a lesson to be learned for any future imprints. In the meantime, Arthur had to focus on recovering the recording.

Chapter 27

Vic didn't sleep a wink. She sat up in bed to a peaceful beauty next to her. If it weren't for the nightmare she was living in, it would be the most beautiful sight in her world. But there was only dread in Vic's heart now. Lying next to the love of her life yet she never felt more alone.

Vic held out no hope for her future and no plan to save herself from it. Arthur Murdoch had won.

As Vic washed her hands in the bathroom sink she stared into the mirror reminiscent of that fateful morning when she recalled Marion's murder. A murder she now knows she didn't commit but none of that mattered anymore. The police were after her. The proof she had of Murdoch's guilt was lost in digital oblivion. She had welcomed love into her life and soon it would be gone forever. Vic suddenly realized if only she hadn't run away from Janey months ago, she would have never met Marion and her life would not be in ruins. Now she has taken Janey down with her. If the cops found out Janey was helping her, she could face criminal charges too.

Vic opened the medicine cabinet to get an aspirin only to find Janey's mom's prescription for Xanax. Vic got queasy looking at them, remembering her own experience with them. She picked up the bottle, it was almost full. *Enough to kill me*, Vic thought.

A panicky voice shot out from the bedroom, "Vic! Where are you?"

Vic put the bottle back in the cabinet and went into the bedroom. She laid her head on Janey's chest while Janey stroked her hair in silence. There were no words for the hopelessness they were both feeling.

Janey made coffee and brought it to Vic who hadn't left the bed. Janey opened a can of worms when she dared to utter the next question. "What do we do now?"

In a slow droning voice Vic replied. "I see three options. Continue to hide out until the cops find me. Turn myself in and hope they believe me or run like the fuckin' wind. Or the 4th option, none of the above."

Janey was puzzled. "What do you mean?"

Vic didn't want to tell her but felt compelled to do so. "End it all."

"Stop!" Janey shouted. "Don't you dare do that to me. Any choice is better than that one."

"I'm sorry, I'm sorry. It's just that..." Vic trailed off.

"Maybe going to the police isn't such a bad idea." Janey was trying to sound upbeat. "Give them the evidence we have."

"We don't have any evidence!" Vic said sharply.

Janey wanted to refute that but she knew Vic was

right. Maybe they could prove Arthur was with her at the bar that night, and they could prove he didn't call Uber but that was hardly a smoking gun.

"You're right," Janey said excitedly. "Let's run. Butch and Sundance. On the road. Live and love all over the world. You and me, babe."

"Again with the us. I can't drag you down with me. You aren't in trouble now, but you would be if you came with me."

"Haven't you figured this out yet, Vic? I love you. It's you and me in this together. I mean in *everything* together, if you'll have me."

Normally, this would be the time Vic ran away as fast as she could, and while she still planned on running, it was for a completely different reason. If it weren't for this mess she was in, she would be all into this relationship. Vic knew she was in love, and it couldn't have happened at a worse time.

"I love you too, and that's why I can't let you give up your life to live as a fugitive with me." By not responding immediately Vic knew Janey had misgivings.

"I don't care," Janey said defiantly.

"Yes you do."

It took a little more discussion before Janey resigned herself to being the helper in Vic's exodus. "I know somebody who can help with a new identity for you. I knew her from when I worked at the women's shelter. She could get ID's for women trying to escape their abuser."

Janey threw in one last attempt to sway Vic, "I could get two, one for each of us."

Vic frowned, "C'mon, we settled this. The cops will be after me till the day I die."

"I know, I know, but I don't have to like it."

They spent the next few hours making plans for Vic's escape.

Afterward Vic said sternly, anticipating an objection, "I have to go see my mother. I have to say goodbye."

As expected, Janey balked but only mildly. She didn't really expect her to skip town without a word to her mother, however rocky the relationship may be.

Chapter 28

Three days later Vic was ready to get off the grid and go into hiding permanently. But first she had to go see her mother.

Janey pulled up to Mary Campo's small, bungalow style home in the suburbs. She scanned the street for police cars, marked or unmarked, but didn't see any. All she saw was a beat up old red pickup truck and a kid on a bicycle. She parked in the driveway, looking about as she exited the car. She nodded and Vic sat up after lying down on the back seat. They quickly made their way in the front door.

A young woman straightened up and snapped a couple of photos of Vic and Janey from inside her truck.

Mary Campo greeted her daughter with an unexpected embrace. Vic was surprised by the hug and by the tears that flowed from both of them. Vic was fearful for her mom and Janey so she kept the visit short. Vic walked out the door without checking to see if the coast was clear. At this point, her concern for her own safety was

"

minimal. But no one came rushing to arrest her and they left.

The emotional visit took a toll on Vic and Janey as neither noticed a beat-up pickup truck following them.

Arthur got a phone call from his investigator with good news. She had found Victoria Campo. Arthur wished he could pick up the phone and call the police, but as long as Campo had the recording, that would be ill-advised. Instead he had his investigator come to his office. He gave her a small package and sent her off on a very special delivery.

When the doorbell rang Vic and Janey nearly jumped out of their seats. They sat still as statues hoping the unwanted guest would simply go away. Then the doorbell rang again. By the time it rang a third time they knew they could no longer ignore it. Janey opened the door just enough to see a thirty-something woman in a Polo shirt and jeans carrying an overstuffed manila envelope.

She didn't look like a cop but Janey was wary just the same. "I've got a package for you," the young woman announced.

"For me?" Janey wanted nothing to do with any package from a stranger. "For Lydia Newcombe?" Janey was thinking it could be something her mother ordered weeks ago.

"Nope, it's for your friend Victoria Campo."

Janey tried to maintain her composure. "Why would you bring me a package for her, she doesn't live here."

"She does right now," she said with a smirk. "Listen, she's gonna want this. It's from Arthur Murdoch."

Janey tried to imagine what Murdoch had sent. She envisioned a severed finger for some morbid reason. Janey took the package despite her misgivings.

Victoria and Janey stared at the package, curious but afraid to open it. Before either mustered up the courage to open it, music started emanating from the bubble wrapped parcel. It sounded like a ring tone. Vic ripped the envelope open to discover it was as expected, a phone. Vic answered it without saying hello.

"Hello Victoria. Peekaboo, I see you."

It was a sinister voice that Vic recognized as Arthur Murdoch. Vic looked around as if she would see him in the corner or at the front door.

"I know you're there Victoria, so we should talk." Arthur was serious now.

"What do you want, Murdoch?" Vic's voice was shaking.

"I would like to make a mutually beneficial arrangement. You have something I want, I have something you want."

"I can't see where you could have anything I could possibly want."

"Perhaps you can't see, but you can hear"

"Victoria honey," Mary Campo's voice was trembling. "This man is scaring me. I don't..." She was cut off.

Hearing her mother's voice tapped into a powerful anger that had been suppressed by fear throughout this whole ordeal. "What have you done to my mother? If you hurt her...I will kill you! Let me talk to her."

"She's fine. I'm fine. We're all fine...if you make the right choice and bring me the recording."

Vic gathered herself. She knew the recording was worthless but she also knew it was the only card she had to play.

"Fine, the recording is yours, but if there is so much as a bruise on my mother's body, I will drive this recorded confession of yours to the police station myself." And she meant it. "You obviously know where I am so come on over and we'll do this. But leave my mother out of this."

"I don't think so," Arthur snickered. "No, you come over to your mother's house. Oh, did I forget to mention that's where I am. Just sitting here having a cold lemonade, me and Mom."

"Stop it!" Vic yelled. "I'm on my way."

"Excellent, Miss Campo. Your mom is so happy to hear that."

Vic and Janey had been planning for days and were just about set. As Vic hung up the phone, Janey grabbed her arm and said, "We'll put our plans off till tomorrow."

"No! Now more than ever, I have to run. You know as soon as he finds out the recording is no good he'll call the cops."

"Speaking of which, how do you plan to fool him about the recording?" Janey asked.

"Easy, play the first 30 seconds that we have and turn

it off. Make the switch for Mom and run like crazy. I don't think he'll come after me, he wants the cops to find me. All he needs is for the tape to be empty. Besides I don't really have a choice. I have to make this work."

When Vic walked into her mother's house they were sitting at the kitchen table with glasses of lemonade, just as Murdoch said. He calmly invited her to sit down with him, which Vic promptly did. All the conflicts through all the years melted away with one embrace between mother and daughter.

"Lovely, yes, hugs. Aren't you two cute?" Arthur said in a sarcastically sappy voice. "But I'm not here for a moving family reunion. Where is the tape?"

Victoria pulled out the recorder from her pocket but kept it in her hand. "Now my mother leaves. This is just between us."

"How do I know that's the recording?" Arthur inquired.

"Let's listen, shall we?" Placing her thumb on the play button, Vic pressed down. She quickly moved her thumb to the stop button knowing exactly how long she had before her ruse would be discovered. But it was unnecessary.

"Stop!" Arthur said sharply. Apparently, Arthur did not want another living soul to hear his confession. "Now hand it over." Arthur pulled the drapes open just a tad and peeked outside.

"I'm alone, but I'm not leaving alone. Mom, get in my car."

Mary Campo got up to leave and to Vic's surprise, Arthur did not object.

"Perhaps we'll meet again, Mrs. Campo." Arthur said with faux politeness.

Vic didn't look back. She took her mother by the arm and headed out the front door. Before she could step out onto the porch she heard the sirens. They were getting closer by the second. Vic looked back at the house and saw Arthur looking out the picture window, smiling ear to ear.

Vic hustled her mother into the car and sped away. Before she made the corner she could see the flashing lights about a quarter mile behind her. Vic raced down the boulevard weaving recklessly between cars. After a close call with a minivan, Vic looked over to see her mother, ghostly white with both hands braced on the dashboard. Vic felt intensely guilty that she was driving like a madwoman with her mother as a passenger. Vic whipped into the McDonald's and pulled around back.

"Get out now," Vic said a little too forcefully.

Mom didn't hesitate. "I love you, Vic," was all she said as she hopped out of the car.

In that moment, all Vic could think about was that her mother had finally called her Vic and not Victoria. But that moment passed as Vic saw an exit to a back street. She briefly paused as three cop cars went blazing past the McDonald's. Vic snuck out the back exit driving cautiously but with haste. Her destination was clear but her path was not. Janey was waiting for her at the abandoned boat launch on the other side of the Missouri River, their escape plan at the ready. But being chased by the police was not part of the plan.

Vic had to get on the highway. There are no side streets that cross over a river the size of the Missouri. Driven by love, Vic plotted her route. Love for Janey, love for freedom. She had to see Janey one more time. It would likely be the last time but she wanted that one last time. She had never wanted any anything this badly in her entire life.

The side street ran parallel to the boulevard but she would have to cut back over to access the highway. With no police in sight Vic turned onto the main drag just short of the highway turn. Afraid to slow down, Vic ran the red light, fortunately safely, and turned onto the highway.

Vic drove as fast as she dared. She would not go quietly. There would be no slow moving White Bronco, OJ style chase. Besides, she wasn't a celebrity, the cops would just shoot her. Vic snickered at the silliness of her own train of thought.

Four exits to go.

The coast was clear. Vic felt so lucky to have found Janey again. Despite her predicament they had managed to find joy in each other. Leaving Janey was the hardest part of her decision to run. On more than one occasion Vic had selfishly wished that Janey was going with her. But because she loved her, she had to do her best to keep her safe from the fallout.

Three exits to go.

Janey was waiting at the boat launch. Their plan was simple. The boat launch was old and unused now, over grown with brush at the edge of the woods. Out of the way, no witnesses. There were personal items in the car and a suicide note was in the mail. It hurt to do it but she had to send it to her mother, she was the logical choice. All that was left was to push her car in the river and let it sink. The little clues she left in the suicide note should lead the cops right to her car.

Meanwhile she'll be on the road in Lydia's car. Vic hadn't decided between hiding in the mountains of Colorado or hiding in the crowds on the streets of New York. East or west, north or south, Vic would decide when the moment came. She also left all her clothes and sundries behind. Dead people don't need those things, or any things, for that matter. She was leaving town with the clothes on her back and money she got from Janey. She hated taking money from Janey but emptying her bank account would be suspicious. Lastly, she left her favorite photo of her with her mother near the river's edge.

Two exits to go.

Vic saw the flashing lights and heard the sirens simultaneously. She passed the last exit before the bridge and was hopeful but hope was lost in an instant. More police had gotten on the highway behind her but it was the blockade of stopped police vehicles at the other end of the bridge that put an end to Vic's journey. Traffic came to a halt and Vic was trapped. She instinctively jumped out of the car intent on running but there was no place to run. There were no options left, save one. She could make the false storyline of suicide a reality. She climbed onto the railing, holding onto a truss, and stared at the massive river below. It was beautiful and frightening and a long way down.

"Victoria Campo. Step off the railing and get down on the ground. NOW!" the uniform officer bellowed.

Vic didn't move. Slowly a woman approached who Vic recognized from their brief encounter at the bar.

"Ms. Campo. Nobody's going to shoot you. Just come down and we can talk." Bailey said in the calmest of voices. "I don't think you really want to die. I know your loved ones want you to live. Think of them."

"I'm innocent. I didn't kill Marion!" Vic felt compelled to scream it to the world.

"I'm inclined to believe you but I need to hear your side of the story," Bailey replied.

This surprised Vic and suddenly she thought about trying to explain herself. Then she remembered how crazy her side of the story was.

"C'mon, let's talk. Suicide isn't the answer," Bailey pleaded.

"No, it isn't," Vic said under her breath. And with that she jumped.

Chapter 29

Bailey lunged at Campo hoping to grab her, but it was too late. "Call River Rescue," Bailey commanded the nearby officer.

"You really think that she survived?" Schwartz asked.

"No, but I want a body. This case needs a body to close it."

Bailey and Schwartz drove down to the base port for River Rescue and awaited word. It was getting darker by the minute which was making recovery difficult.

Janey couldn't help but notice the flashing lights on the bridge in the distance. She had a bad feeling in her gut. Fortunately, she brought binoculars to scout out the area for privacy. Her worst nightmare came true when she spotted Vic standing on the bridge, surrounded by police. Actually, her worst nightmare came true moments later when she saw her love leap to her certain death. Janey gasped and crumbled to her knees in shock. Janey sat down and tears poured down her face. She knew this relationship was doomed, but hope springs eternal and that is what she had until a minute ago.

Vic hit the water hard and painfully. She started flailing in desperation, frantically trying to reach the surface. Her body was out of control but her mind only had thoughts of Janey. Her body relaxed, her heart slowed as she accepted her fate. That lasted for seconds before she realized that was exactly what she needed to do, relax and go with the current. She found her way to the surface and allowed her body to float down the river. When the time was right she rolled over onto her stomach and began to swim at a diagonal toward the shore. As she approached the shore it became more and more elusive. The current was strong but Vic was stronger. She reached the wooded shore, short of breath and exhausted. It seemed like she had been swimming for miles. Darkness had fallen quickly but the lights of the police cars still shone bright in the distance.

Vic got off the shore as soon as she could will her wet, weak body to move. Heading away from the bridge was the point, finding Janey was the goal. Vic suddenly worried that Janey had given up and left. If she knew Vic had jumped she was probably cursing her name as well.

Under cover of darkness, Vic stumbled through the woods, trying to see but not be seen, as she made her way to the rendezvous point.

A broken hearted Janey gathered herself and climbed into her car. She began backing out to turn around when her headlights shone on a figure coming out of the woods. Janey thought she was hallucinating at first, but there before her stood a wet and dirty Victoria Campo. A sight to behold, Janey got out of her car and wrapped her arms around her. To Janey, it was if she had risen from the grave. The two embraced and wept, showering each other with kisses for what seemed to be an eternity.

Finally Janey broke the silence, "Baby, you scared me to death. I thought you were...dead. How? Oh, who cares. You're safe and that's all that matters."

"Let's get out of here, Janey."

"I brought you some clothes, you can change in the car."

"I thought I was leaving all my clothes to support the suicide scam. Oh yeah, that story is kinda blown to hell now, isn't it?"

"Well, if they know your intent was suicide all along they might be more inclined to believe you succeeded. Besides nobody is going to notice a couple of tee shirts and some jeans are missing from your wardrobe of a hundred tee shirts and jeans." Janey smiled and Vic was impressed she could make a joke in the midst of this bedlam.

Janey had brought her mother's car in accordance with their original plan. They were going to push Vic's car into the river, call the police anonymously as a witness and leave in Lydia's car.

They had switched the plates, back to the original cars, earlier in the day so as not to be trying to do it in the dark at the boat launch. Their plan was voided but the suicide theory has now become doubly convincing.

The reality of the situation was once again settling in with Janey.   Her love was found and now would be lost again forever.

"Now what?" Janey said curiously.

"Now we go on like we planned. I'll disappear and you'll be safe and live your life. Hopefully, you'll find someone to share it with."

"No, don't you see? Your mom is a witness to Murdoch's treachery. You don't have to run!" Janey said excitedly.

In all the excitement Vic had failed to realize that possibility. But she was not convinced. "Except what did she witness? Murdoch didn't have a gun to her head or a knife to her throat. He never verbally threatened her. She invited him into the house. He never harmed her or held her against her will. For crying out loud, she served him lemonade. In the end, he didn't even try to stop her from leaving with me."

"Yes, in the end, but she witnessed the whole exchange for the recording. That has to count for something."

"Count for what?" Vic questioned. "He was the one who called the police. He could claim he was just trying to catch me because the police had failed to do so." As if she were Murdoch, Vic continued, "I was there just talking to her mother when Vic showed up, and I called the cops as soon as I could. The woman murdered my wife, I just wanted her caught." Vic continued, "And the recording...what recording? I wouldn't have an ounce of proof that one existed. Just me and my mother's word."

Much as she didn't want to agree, Janey knew Vic had a point. "So you're not willing to even try talking to the police with your mom?"

"No. Besides, I just ran from the cops and jumped off and bridge. If they assume I'm dead, the stage is all set for me to run."

"Please, I'm begging you." Tears rolled down Janey's cheek.

"You know I have to go. It's the only way to keep you and Mom safe."

"Stop it! Don't go spouting some noble nonsense to me. I know what has to be done, but let's keep things real." Janey began to sob.

Vic tried to comfort her, stroking her hair and back as she drove. It didn't seem to help, but she couldn't give Janey what she wanted and they both knew it.

"Where are you taking us, sweetie? This isn't safe for you." Vic spoke with a tinge of fear in her voice.

"I don't know, just away from here."

"I have to drop you off somewhere then I have to leave town, pronto," Vic said solemnly.

"Maybe you could hide in town for a few days to see how things shake out with your mom and the police. It's worked so far."

"Uh, no it hasn't. Murdoch found me and probably would again." Vic repeated herself, "I have to go and I have to go now!"

Janey made a sudden jerk of the wheel and they were pulling into the casino parking lot. "Might as well drop me here. I can catch a cab here," Janey said angrily.

Vic could hear the anger in her voice so she clasped her hand over Janey's clenched fist and said, "I know it's not what you want. It's not what I want either. But it's what we must do. I love you with all my heart. You are my everything. I'm sorry for what I've put you through. I'm sorry for what I'll put you through after I'm gone. If there was another way..." Vic stopped, at a loss for what to say next.

"I know," Janey said softly. They kissed and cried and said their goodbyes. Janey exited the car. Vic dried the tears from her eyes as she waved her last farewell and drove away in the darkness.

Vic pulled up to a dingy motel off the beaten path. She was exhausted. The chase, the jump, the swim and saying goodbye to the best thing that had ever happened in her life, left her tired and unable to drive. It was risky stopping this close to the city but it was unavoidable. She had her fake ID for the hotel but she had originally planned on making it south to Memphis by morning. Vic got a room and turned on the TV, wondering if she made the news, but it was much too late to catch any news.

Vic's head was filled with fearful thoughts. She feared for her own safety but mostly she feared for her mother and Janey. If the police discovered Janey's involvement she could land in jail. They might get her to tell them that Vic was alive, and more. Oddly enough,

Vic hoped that Janey would tell them what they wanted to know if it kept her out of prison.

Then there were the feelings of anger. Murdoch had killed Marion and maybe more. He had threatened her mother. Vic knew she was the only one who knew what he was, and still is. In her mind, only she could stop him.

It was a fitful night of little sleep. Guilt, fear and anger prevailed. In the early dawn, Vic went outside to get to the front desk for coffee. She saw a man who looked a lot like Arthur Murdoch get into his car. She chased after the car on foot until he was long out of sight. Vic immediately wondered if he had been there to do his magic trick of hypnosis. She began to panic, however she had no unfamiliar memories in her head. Still, she knew she was as vulnerable as countless others.

Vic told herself it couldn't be him, he couldn't have found her. Then she thought of the burner phone Arthur had sent her. She still had it with her. Vic wondered if he could have tracked her by way of the phone. This sent a whole new wave of fear through Vic's body. She grabbed her bag and headed out on the next step of her journey. After getting on the highway Vic tossed the phone out the window with an emphatic, "Track that, mother fucker!"

Vic drove for hours, stopping only for gas. Her mind was in constant turmoil. She stopped at another nameless motel for the night.

Everywhere she looked she saw Arthur Murdoch. At the motel office, the homeless guy on the street, the guy in the car she passed on the highway, her mind was playing tricks on her, and she knew it.

She knew he would not stop hunting her. He would question the suicide. He would not stop killing. How many others would he destroy with his gimmick and a gun? These thoughts permeated her mind as exhaustion took over and she fell asleep.

With each passing mile Vic felt more and more guilty. She was taking her life on the road, far away from Murdoch, but leaving Janey and her mother in the same town with the psychopath. He would be angry that his patsy had not been neatly captured and convicted. If the police questioned her suicide, so would he. Then he might revert to threatening her mother again just to see if Vic showed up to save her. And he may see her mother as a witness and a threat. Suddenly Vic realized that even though she didn't see her mother as a valuable witness, Murdoch might. Or a similar scenario viewing Janey as someone who knew too much. There was no end to his madness and it was unfair to leave her loved ones in extreme danger. Vic had to stop driving, she was too unnerved. She grabbed lunch at a diner and headed north on the interstate. That night Vic accepted the fact that sleep was unattainable. Things as they were equated to a Murdoch victory.

Vic wept and shook until she found the courage to accept the path that her life was on.

Chapter 30

The next day Vic woke to a familiar feeling, memories that seemed unreal.

She crept quietly, baseball bat in hand, to stand beside him as he lay in bed. With all the courage she could muster, she slammed the bat square on his head. His body convulsed for a moment then his eyes opened. She braced herself for another blow, but with him looking at her she couldn't do it. He rolled out of the bed and struggled to his feet. Vic retreated into the hall. The man came towards her. Vic waved the bat in a threatening manner but he wasn't fazed in the least. His gait was unsteady and in a flash Vic lunged at him and threw him over the railing. He landed on the lower floor, head first, motionless. Vic gathered herself and walked down the stairs. She stood over the bloody body and stared into the unmistakable face of Arthur Murdoch.

Vic stood in the bathroom of what would surely be the first in a long line of rundown motels as a fugitive. She splashed water on her face and stared at the mirror. Her hands shook at the realization she once more remembered committing a murder.

Only this time was different. These memories were crystal clear and they were all her own. Arthur Murdoch would kill no more. Vic smiled knowing her loved ones were now safe.